THE D

Speech therapist Meryl Taylor was furious when Dr Gareth Owen-Thomas got the job as senior doctor at the Wellford Centre—especially when he told her that he intended to run the centre efficiently—with or without her help! It was bad enough being forced to work with the fiery Welsh doctor—without finding she was expected to *live* with him!

Sarah Franklin lives in Cambridgeshire with her husband, cat and a 'very bossy but lovable' dog. She has always been interested in anything medical. Both her daughters, before marriage, were working in the field of medicine; one as a nurse, the other as an aesthetician, and Sarah herself has been a keen member of the St John Ambulance Brigade and holds their certificates for nursing and first aid. Writing and researching the medical content of her books takes up most of her time, but her hobbies include gardening, the theatre and music as well as 'dabbling with a paint brush'. *The Doctor from Wales* is Sarah Franklin's twelfth Doctor Nurse Romance.

THE DOCTOR FROM WALES

BY
SARAH FRANKLIN

MILLS & BOON LIMITED
15–16 BROOK'S MEWS
LONDON W1A 1DR

First published in Great Britain 1986
by Mills & Boon Limited

© Sarah Franklin 1986

Australian copyright 1986
Philippine copyright 1986

ISBN 0 263 75374 3

Set in 10 on 12 pt Linotron Times
03–0486–52,300

Photoset by Rowland Phototypesetting Limited
Bury St Edmunds, Suffolk
Made and printed in Great Britain by
Richard Clay (The Chaucer Press) Limited
Bungay, Suffolk

CHAPTER ONE

IT was a beautiful mellow September evening, golden with late sunshine. Bees buzzed in the last of the purple clematis flowers on the sun-warmed wall of Dr Margaret's cottage and a sleepy butterfly hovered over the buddleia by the gate. But all this idyllic peace was wasted on Meryl as she leaned heavily on the doorbell. She was fuming. Her weekend in London was completely spoiled. She had gone to spend a couple of days with Moira, an old friend from college days, on her aunt's suggestion—to 'recharge the batteries', as she put it. Now it was all too clear why she had wanted to get her out of the way—so that she and her committee could appoint this total stranger behind her back! Wellford House Health Centre being run by a doctor from out of town—out of the county—even out of the *country*! The local people would never stand for it. *She* would never stand for it, and she was here to tell her aunt just that!

She took her finger off the doorbell as her aunt's form could be seen through the frosted glass panel of the door, and a moment later it was opened to reveal the startled face of Dr Margaret Taylor.

'Good gracious, it's you! I thought the four-minute warning must have gone without my hearing it!'

If Meryl hadn't been so preoccupied with annoyance she would have noticed that her aunt was looking particularly attractive. Her silver hair was newly set and she wore the blue dress that brought out the colour of her still beautiful eyes. She had even put on some make-up and a little pale pink nail varnish. Oblivious to all this, Meryl brushed past her into the hall, her cheeks pink and her amber eyes flashing.

'I've just heard,' she announced breathlessly. 'I found your note when I got back from London—'

'Oh yes, your weekend. Did you enjoy it, dear?' Margaret interrupted blandly.

'What?—Oh yes, but it's completely ruined now!'

Margaret looked sympathetic. 'Really? Why is that?'

Meryl threw up her hands exasperatedly. 'That's just what I'm trying to tell you! You only sent me away so that I wouldn't try to talk you into anything, didn't you? You knew all along that I wanted Richard to get this job. He really deserved it, yet you appoint this—this—*foreigner*! What on earth do you think the patients will make of it? You know how conservative they are. You must have let the others talk you into it. I thought you agreed with me about Richard.' She paused for breath, and Margaret frowned at her.

'Suppose we talk about this in the morning, Meryl?'

'I want to talk about it now!'

'I really can't think why you're so angry.' Margaret lowered her voice to a whisper. 'I agree that Richard seemed a likely candidate, but Dr Owen-Thomas is ideal, as you'll see for yourself when you meet him. He isn't a foreigner, as you put it, he's from South Wales —and I must say I'm surprised at your biased view.'

'How can you say that?' Meryl argued. 'The patients won't be able to understand a word he's saying. It'll be a disaster. You know how they hate anything unfamiliar. Besides—Welsh!—before we know it he'll be starting a male voice choir and spouting Dylan Thomas at us!' She paused, wondering why her aunt's face had turned so red, then a voice behind her made her start.

'I only know one line of Dylan Thomas, so that shouldn't take long—and I can't sing for toffee.'

She spun round and found herself face to face with a powerfully built man who was leaning against the sitting room door. He was dark—so dark that the growth of beard under his skin was visible even though he had recently shaved. Meryl didn't trust men as dark as that, she told herself. His dark grey eyes appraised her with interest, taking in the tall, slim figure in the green linen suit; the mass of auburn hair and the flashing amber-green eyes. For a moment they stared at each other, then he stepped forward. 'Please allow me to introduce myself—Dr Gareth Owen-Thomas.'

Dr Margaret quickly put in: 'This is my niece, Meryl Taylor. She's our speech therapist. You'll be working together under the same roof—some of the time, any-way—' She trailed off lamely as she looked from Meryl's hostile face to the doctor's amused one.

'*Really*—a speech therapist, is she?' One dark eye-brow rose cynically. 'I thought she must be the County MOH at the very least!'

Meryl coloured as the barb went home. Clearly he had overheard her remarks. Well, what did it matter? He might as well know where he stood from the very beginning. She turned towards the door, but Margaret said quickly:

'Don't go, Meryl. Gareth and I were just about to have tea. You will stay and join us, won't you?'

Meryl stared at her aunt disbelievingly. So he was 'Gareth' already, was he? No doubt he was calling her Margaret too. How cosy! 'No, thank you,' she said stiffly. 'I have my unpacking to do. The weekend was rather hectic and I have a full day tomorrow, so I'm going to have an early night.'

Margaret accompanied her out on to the porch. 'I'll explain everything in the morning,' she said quietly. 'Please don't look so angry, Meryl. Gareth is quite clearly the wisest choice we could have made. In fact I'd go as far as to say that we're very lucky to get him.'

'How lovely for us! It's obvious that you're smitten with him!' Meryl made to move away, but her aunt laid a hand on her arm.

'First thing in the morning, Meryl—in my office.' Meryl saw that the smile had left her aunt's face. 'I want to speak to you before surgery starts, so don't be late.' Her voice was firm. 'There's quite a lot I want to say to you.'

Meryl slammed the gate behind her and got into the car, revving the engine noisily. When her aunt's face took on that look she knew she was beaten; there would be no moving her. Angrily she toyed with the idea of applying for another job, away from Millington, the sleepy little East Coast town where she had grown up—away from all the people who knew her so well—*too* well.

Dr Margaret's cottage stood on the outskirts of the town and Meryl drove back along the coast road. Once it had been little more than a sandy track, dotted with holiday bungalows and shops selling buckets and spades, ice-cream and postcards. Shops that in winter were closed and shuttered against the harsh, icy North Sea winds. Now the road was smooth and wide. The holiday bungalows had gone, to be replaced by a new estate of houses built to accommodate the newcomers—the 'gas people', as the locals called them. This estate was only one of many that had sprung up over the last few years. When the gas rig had appeared, like some science-fiction monster, grown up almost overnight out of the sea, life had changed in Millington; the town had grown by leaps and bounds, a false, mushroom kind of growth that the local people understandably found difficult to come to terms with.

Dr Gilbert Taylor, Meryl's grandfather, had been concerned about it. The local cottage hospital could not adequately cope with the new influx of patients, and long before his death he had formed the plan that was now being put into operation. Wellford House, the large Georgian house that had been the Taylor family home for over two hundred years, was to become the town's new health centre. Dr Gilbert's dream, of all the doctors as well as the periphery branches of medicine being housed under one roof, was at last coming to fruition. At this moment the builders were putting the finishing touches to the extension that had been built at the rear of the building, and on the previous Friday a new senior doctor had been appointed: Dr Gareth Owen-Thomas.

As Meryl drove back to Wellford House, where she still occupied the small flat under the eaves, she fumed afresh about the new appointment. When Aunt Margaret had announced that she felt she was too old to take up the post of senior doctor at the centre, Meryl had been sure that Richard would get it. Richard Jessel and she had been friends since schooldays. He had been a qualified doctor for four years now, for three of which he had been a member of the group practice at Wellford House. As her thoughts stayed with him she found herself automatically heading the car towards the road where he lived. Poor Richard, elbowed out to make way for this upstart foreigner!

But when Richard answered the door to her urgent ring he didn't look at all concerned. He wore jeans and a sweater and his hair was tousled. He was just about to open a can of beer and make himself a sandwich, he told her. He had been relaxing with his records on his first Sunday evening off for weeks.

'A good thing when this new chap starts,' he called out from the kitchen. 'We can certainly do with another pair of hands in the practice. That'll make four of us, not counting old Dr Henderson over on the other side of town, but I doubt if he'll ever be persuaded to join us at the Wellford Centre.'

Meryl stood in the doorway, regarding him with raised eyebrows. 'You couldn't care less, could you?' she asked incredulously. 'Don't you care about this Owen-Thomas person being appointed over your head?'

He turned to look at her with a grin. 'Not a bit. You win some—you lose some. He seems a nice bloke, and anyway he's older than me—had far more experience.' He handed her a thickly cut ham sandwich on a plate. 'As far as I can make out he's worked in mining areas ever since he qualified. He's used to working in industrial communities. There's no doubt that he's the right man for the job. Besides, I'm not altogether sure that I'm ready for that kind of responsibility yet.'

Meryl shook her head. 'I simply don't understand you. Haven't you any ambition?'

'Of course I have. But I've all my life ahead of me, and I'd like to enjoy myself a little first before I get into a job of that weight. Of course, if I'd landed the job I'd have buckled down, but I didn't—so why worry?'

'Well, I'm sorry, but I think that's a rather feeble attitude,' Meryl told him bluntly. 'Personally I think they've made a mistake. I can't see the locals taking to this Welshman. You know what they are—they simply don't trust outsiders.'

Richard smiled. 'I think you're a little out of date on that, love. After all, nine tenths of the population are what you call outsiders now, and on the whole I believe the natives have stood up to the changes pretty well. I can't see that one Welsh doctor is going to stand the place on its ear—especially one who's so obviously gifted.'

Meryl sighed and sat down to eat her sandwich. It looked as though she was outnumbered, but even so, she wouldn't change her mind easily. Time would tell. They chatted for a while about Meryl's weekend, then Richard said suddenly:

'Look, Meryl—you say that the local people won't take to this change. Are you sure it's not you?'

She stared at him. 'I don't know what you mean.'

He frowned. 'Don't take what I'm going to say the wrong way, but imagine how much say you'd have in the situation if you were working in any other place. I mean, being related to the two main doctors in the town has—has—' He searched for the words, but Meryl broke in to supply them:

'Spoilt me? Made me too big for my boots?'

He sighed. 'Well, I wouldn't have put it quite so bluntly, but you wouldn't have felt as free to express your opinion if you hadn't been Dr Margaret's niece, now would you?'

She was silent, thinking of Gareth Owen-Thomas's remark when he had learned that she was a speech therapist. 'I thought she must be the County MOH at the very least!' Now that she had calmed down she realised how very rude and spoilt she must have sounded, but she didn't care. It was all too clear that he needed putting in his place anyhow. He had that maddening air of self-confidence oozing from every pore. Obviously he had been idolised and revered in his little mining village; put on a pedestal like some kind of god. Well, he'd soon learn that she wasn't so easily impressed!

Suddenly something occurred to her. 'Is he married?' she asked Richard. He shook his head.

'Can't be. I heard him asking Margaret about a place to live and he said that anything would do as long as he could be on his own.'

'There you are, then!' Meryl said triumphantly. 'You know yourself that the patients expect a senior GP to be married—especially the female ones.'

Richard grinned mischievously. 'Maybe it won't be long before he is! I daresay he'll be setting a few hearts a-flutter with those macho good looks of his, wouldn't you say?'

She shrugged. 'Personally I think he's rather coarse-looking.'

Richard smiled wryly. 'Well, I suggest you take another look when you're not feeling quite so resentful, though I'm not complaining if you prefer me, of course.' He went to the door with her. 'Heavy day tomorrow?'

She nodded. 'Clinic at St Luke's in the morning and some ward visits; a combined clinic at Northwich in the afternoon, then I have a new patient to see on the way back if I'm not too late. I was planning to get in an early night.'

He kissed her briefly. 'Off you go, then. And try not to worry too much about the new boss. I daresay you'll like him well enough once he's settled in.'

She lifted her shoulders. 'Thank goodness *that's* not obligatory!'

At Wellford House she parked the car in the spacious garage at the rear and used her key to let herself into the house. Everywhere there was evidence of the builders, the smell of new wood, putty, paint and varnish. Most of the work had been completed now, but there were still a few odd jobs to be done—doors to hang and the decorating to finish. Soon the builders would be moving out to make way for carpet fitters. The centre was scheduled to open officially on the first of November. The ceremony was to be performed by the local MP and covered by the regional TV station.

Meryl climbed the three flights of stairs to her flat. She had lived there since she returned to Millington as a qualified speech therapist; the conversion of the three attic rooms had been her grandfather's surprise present to her. She loved the little flat with its dormer windows that looked out over the town towards the sea. On winter nights as she lay tucked up in bed, she could listen to the wind in the treetops, and in summer, with all the windows wide open, she could smell the salty tang of the sea and hear the distant cry of gulls. She made herself a hot drink and went to bed, falling asleep almost at once, tired after the drive from London and her emotional outburst.

She had no idea of the time, or of what had awakened her. She lay blinking into the darkness for a moment, then she heard the noise. It was downstairs. She stiffened—someone was in the house! Switching on her bedside lamp, she looked at the alarm clock, but it had stopped; she must have forgotten to wind it before she went to sleep. Getting out of bed, she tiptoed to the door and listened—yes, there it was again—footsteps echoing on the bare boards below. Her heart hammered as she dialled Richard's number. As he lifted the receiver she could hear the strains of a Beethoven symphony in the background. Obviously he was having a late session.

'Hello, Dr Jessel speaking.'

'Richard—' she tried hard not to sound too panicky, 'there's someone in the house—downstairs. I can hear them!'

'All right—stay where you are, I'll be right over.' He had hung up before she had time to say anything else, and immediately she wished she hadn't rung him. It could be nothing—one of the builders, maybe, who had left something behind and come to find it.

She pulled on a dressing gown and took a torch from the kitchen cupboard, then, cautiously opening her door, she crept down the first flight of stairs and stood listening on the landing. Yes—there was the noise again. Someone was definitely moving about on the ground floor—and making no attempt to be quiet about it either. Whoever it was obviously thought they were alone in the house.

Keeping close to the wall, Meryl edged down the next two flights of stairs, her eyes searching the dark corners of the hall. There was no one there; the intruder must be in the new extension at the rear. She pushed open the swing doors leading through to the new consulting rooms and stood quietly in the corridor, her heart thudding—then, slowly, the door to her left began to open. Someone—a man—was coming out of the room.

Her heart in her mouth, Meryl raised the hand that held
the torch and sprang at him, but his reactions were too
quick for her. Sensing the movement, he swung round.
An iron hand closed around her wrist and before she
knew what was happening he had forced her arm halfway up her back, rendering her helpless. The sudden
pain made her cry out as he marched her towards the old
consulting rooms at the front of the house. Once inside
her aunt's surgery he switched on the light.

'Squatters, eh? Now, let's have a look at you—Oh,
good God!'

She found herself looking into the dark, angry eyes of
Dr Owen-Thomas, and her anger exploded.

'What on earth do you think you're doing, creeping
about in the middle of the night and—and—*attacking*
people in their own homes?' she shouted. 'How *dare* you
manhandle me like some criminal?' She rubbed her
bruised arm.

'I'm sorry,' he said abruptly. 'But I wasn't aware that
anyone lived here. Your aunt gave me a key and I was
just having a look round before turning in. It *isn't* the
middle of the night, you know—it's actually only half-
past ten.'

'That's irrelevant,' she snapped. 'I was asleep. I woke
and heard someone. I thought you were a burglar!'

He sat on the edge of Margaret's desk and regarded
her, arms folded, his eyes flickering with amusement. 'In
that case, wasn't it a little foolhardy to come down like
that?' He eyed her bare feet and flimsy dressing gown.
'It's a good job it *was* only me. Here, let me look at that
arm.' He seized her arm unceremoniously and pushed
up the sleeve of her dressing gown, to reveal the ugly
bruise, already darkening at the edges.

'Only a bruise,' he announced dismissively. 'I'm sure you've had worse than that!'

'It hurts,' she said petulantly. 'A lot!'

'What do you want me to prescribe—amputation? Or shall I just kiss it better?' He chuckled maddeningly.

Meryl was so angry at his implication that she was behaving like a child that she felt tears pricking the corners of her eyes and tightening her throat.

'I think you're a perfect swine,' she told him coldly. 'I thought so this evening, and now I know my first impression was right. I—' She broke off as she heard a sudden noise in the hallway, then the door swung open to reveal Richard with two large policemen in tow. He stared from Meryl to Gareth, then back again. Gareth was the first to recover.

'Hello there,' he said welcomingly. 'Come to join the party?'

'Richard—I made a mistake,' Meryl began, her cheeks crimson. 'I thought I heard a burglar moving around down here. I didn't know Aunt Maggie had given Dr Owen-Thomas a key.'

'And I, in the dark, mistook Miss Taylor here for a squatter!' Gareth announced. 'I'm afraid I was a bit rough.' He looked at Meryl, holding up his hands in submission. 'Well, here's your chance. Four strong arms of the law. If you want to give me in charge—'

Richard and the two policemen began to laugh, and Gareth joined in. In front of Meryl's incredulous eyes Richard calmly introduced the Wellford Centre's new senior doctor to the policemen, while she stood there shivering. At last, unnoticed, she left the room to creep back upstairs to bed, her heart filled with loathing and resentment for the new senior doctor from South Wales.

CHAPTER TWO

IT was eight-thirty when Meryl tapped on the door of her aunt's surgery. A cook voice answered:

'Come in.'

Dr Margaret Taylor sat at her desk opening the morning's mail. She looked brisk and efficient, at least ten years younger than her fifty-eight years. She looked up at Meryl with a smile.

'Good morning. I hope you're feeling better now, dear.'

Meryl coloured. 'I'm sorry if I embarrassed you yesterday, but I was so angry about Richard not getting the job.' She sat down opposite her aunt. 'I needn't have worried, though. I went to see Richard after I left you and he really doesn't seem to care one way or another!'

Margaret shook her head, smiling indulgently. 'I've told you before about getting worked up over these causes of yours. It's a fool's game—a waste of energy and emotion most of the time. People do rather tend to like running their own lives, you know.'

Meryl shrugged. She was in no mood for a lecture this morning. She wondered if her aunt could possibly have heard about last night's fiasco yet. 'What was it you wanted to talk to me about?' she asked tentatively.

Dr Margaret pushed aside the pile of mail and leaned forward. 'I just wanted to put you straight about Dr Owen-Thomas,' she said. 'He really is ideal for this job,

17

Meryl. He knows the problems that crop up in an industrial community very thoroughly—the social ones as well as medical. He's had the right kind of experience. Richard himself would be the first to admit that he has a long way to go before he's ready for this kind of responsibility.'

'I know—I know.' Meryl didn't add that she and Richard had already discussed the matter at some length.

'There's another thing,' Margaret went on. 'Although I feel I'm too old for the post myself I have no intention of retiring for some time yet. When the centre opens I shall be taking on most of the obstetric and child care work—you know I've always had a special interest in that field. I shall be doing the ante- and post-natal clinics with the help of Mike Taggart. Gareth will be stand-by doctor for the rig—helping out when the company doctor isn't available or in emergencies.' She glanced at Meryl. 'What I'm trying to say is that we shall all be working in close communication under one roof—each one of us valuable in our own field. You and I may be related, Meryl, but as far as our working relationship goes it counts for nothing. In other words I *don't* want another display like yesterday's.'

'I couldn't possibly have known that Dr Owen-Thomas was with you, could I?' Meryl protested.

'Nevertheless, I'm sure you take my point,' Margaret said firmly. 'The new senior doctor of the Wellford Centre was appointed by an experienced group of people, including myself, and it was quite unforgivable of you to question that appointment. It says a lot for Gareth's good nature that he saw the episode as amusing rather than offensive. I particularly want the working atmosphere to be a happy one. I hope very much that you'll try to get along with him.'

Meryl chewed her lip. It was a long time since her aunt had taken her to task so thoroughly. 'I'm sorry. I'll try.'

'Good.' Margaret began to tidy her letters into neat piles. 'Gareth has already been in to see me this morning. He'll be going back to Wales later today to clear things up before starting his new job here. He's already met the other doctors in the group, of course, and he's trying to see as many of the others as he can too before he goes—especially you. Can I pencil you in for one o'clock?'

'I've got a pretty heavy day—' Meryl started to say, then she noticed her aunt's expression as she peered at her over the tops of her spectacles. 'Oh, all right, I suppose one o'clock will be all right,' she said.

'Marvellous!' Margaret took off her glasses and got up to come round the desk to Meryl. 'You don't mind my being frank with you, do you, dear? It's for your own good, believe me. I'm afraid Father and I rather spoiled you. Working in a small family practice was so cosy, but all that will be changed now.' She smiled sympathetically. 'You still miss him, don't you? So do I. But I know how much this project meant to him, and that's why I'm so determined that nothing shall interfere with its smooth running.'

As Meryl drove to St Luke's Hospital to take her morning clinic she thought about her conversation with her aunt. She was right, of course; it had been presumptuous of her to assume that she could influence the appointment of a new senior doctor. Being the granddaughter of Dr Gilbert Taylor meant nothing. She must prove herself on her own merits, and it was time she made a start. All the same, she wished that the new doctor could have been someone other than the fearsome Gareth Owen-Thomas! Not only had they got off to the worst possible start, but she doubted if they would ever see eye to eye. And what Aunt Maggie would say when she heard about last night, she shuddered to think!

The morning clinic was with children, and as she worked Meryl soon forgot her present worries. Working with the children always fascinated her, and the hospital had recently installed a new Language Master machine so that each child could work with his or her own tape. One four-year-old with a delayed speech problem had improved quite dramatically since he had been working with the machine, and this morning his mother expressed her delight to Meryl.

'I can't tell you how pleased and relieved we are, Miss Taylor.' She smiled. 'Everyone in the family thought that Darren was retarded. I always knew he wasn't, of course, but it's such a relief to prove them wrong. He's saying more words each day now. By the time he goes to school he should have almost caught up.'

After the clinic was over Meryl went up to the men's ward of the cottage hospital where a patient who was recovering from a stroke had been sent from Northwich General. The Ward Sister saw her through the glass panel of her office and came out to meet her.

'I expect you've come to see Mr Johnson. He's in the end bed and making nice progress. His speech is coming back slowly but surely, but he's aphasic. His wife is with him at the moment. If you'd like to have a word with her after you've seen him you can use my office.'

Meryl nodded. 'Thanks. I'm going to need her co-operation.'

Mr Johnson was a tall, good-looking man of about sixty, and Meryl saw at once that Sister had been right. He sat up in bed, listening to what his wife was saying to him with an expression of concentration. She stood at the end of his bed.

'Good morning. I'm Meryl Taylor, the speech therapist. I expect you've been expecting to see me.'

The woman who had been sitting at the bedside stood up. She was small and fair with a faded look that spoke of weeks of worry. She held out her hand. 'Good morning. How do you do.'

'I shall be in to see you each morning from now on to help you with your speech, Mr Johnson,' Meryl explained. 'You can help too, Mrs Johnson. If you have a few minutes to spare now I'll explain how to you.'

In Sister's office she tried to put Mrs Johnson at her ease, inviting her to take a seat while she consulted the patient's notes. 'Your husband is making good progress, she told her. 'We know that he hasn't lost his ability to speak because he can still make sounds such as coughing. His condition is what's known as aphasia. Don't worry about it. Sometimes after a stroke a patient needs this period of silence, so we won't try to hurry him back to normal too quickly. When you talk to him he understands perfectly what you say—I'm sure you can tell that. He knows what he wants to say to you in reply too, but somehow it all gets mixed up—it's a bit like a ball of string that's hopelessly tangled. He'll come out of it all right, but it will take lots of patience on your part and his. Speak to him normally and try to let him know that it doesn't matter how long it takes for him to get his answers out. In the meantime I'll be up each day to help him.'

Mrs Johnson's eyes filled with tears. 'Poor Gerald! He's always been such an articulate man. He used to make such lovely after-dinner speeches—he was President of the Rotary Club, you know. It's terrible to see him like this.'

Meryl smiled reassuringly. 'Don't let him see your distress, though, will you? His recovery will depend a great deal on your attitude. We'll have him making those after-dinner speeches again in time, with a little luck.'

As Meryl was making her way back to Outpatients she ran into Jean Taggart, St Luke's resident physiotherapist. Jean was the wife of Mike Taggart, a member of the Wellford House Group practice. She greeted Meryl warmly.

'Hello there! Been up to see Mr Johnson? I'm on my way up to see him myself, though I hope he'll soon be fit enough to come down and exercise with the others.'

Meryl nodded. 'He seems to be doing very well.'

Jean looked round and lowered her voice. 'Have you met the new senior yet?'

'Yes, I have.'

Jean looked at her. 'Well, what did you think?'

Meryl shrugged. 'I haven't really had a chance to form an opinion,' she said stiffly.

Jean laughed. 'What's the matter with your eyes, girl? He's about the most attractive man we've seen around here for years and you say you 'haven't had time to form an opinion'! He stayed with us over the weekend, you know. The girls were home from school for half-term and they simply couldn't take their eyes off him—it was quite embarrassing! They're just at that age. I shall really have to have a talk with them.'

The Taggarts lived in a rambling Victorian house on

the edge of town, and Meryl remembered Aunt Maggie saying that Jean had offered to put the successful candidate up if he wanted to stay over the weekend. She forced a smile.

'Well, I'm glad you got along with him so well. As a matter of fact I have an appointment to see him at one o'clock, so I'd better be running along if I want to snatch some lunch first.'

'The best of luck, then, though I'm sure you and he will get along like a house on fire,' Jean told her. 'Mind you, I can imagine he has a tough side to him, so watch out for yourself!' She went off down the corridor, chuckling to herself, and Meryl turned away gloomily. Little did Jean—or anyone else—know what she'd already done to incur the disapproval of Dr Owen-Thomas. She'd done more to make herself look foolish over the last twenty-four hours than she'd done in her entire lifetime!

Back at Wellford House Meryl let herself in and picked her way through wood shavings and carpenters' litter, making her way towards the stairs. One of the workmen called out to her:

'Watch yourself, miss. We've got some floorboards up at the bottom of the stairs. They needed replacing, so we thought we'd better get it done before the carpets go down.' He grinned at her. 'Don't worry, another couple of days now and we should be out from under your feet.'

Thanking him for the warning, Meryl picked her way round the hole in the floor and climbed the stairs to make herself a quick snack lunch. She had only eaten half of it when there was a sharp tap on her door and she opened it to find Dr Owen-Thomas standing outside. Her eyebrows rose in surprise.

'Oh! I thought my appointment with you was at one o'clock.'

'It is,' he told her laconically. 'But I have only you to see now. I rather want to get away, so I thought I'd come up to see you here instead.' He peered round her into the flat. 'May I come in?'

Meryl swallowed the food still in her mouth and held the door open. 'Yes, of course. You'll have to excuse me, I'm still having lunch.'

'Please don't mind me—carry on.' He stood looking round her small living room with interest. 'This is very nice, I must say.'

Meryl went through to the kitchen. What cheek! Surely he could have waited another fifteen minutes. She was entitled to a short lunch break in private. As she sat down at the table and returned to her salad he appeared in the doorway, eyeing her speculatively.

'How's the arm?'

She blushed, a forkful of lettuce halfway to her mouth. 'Arm? Oh, it's fine, thank you.'

'Not hurting any more?' He looked amused.

'A little.' She stood up and went to plug in the kettle—mainly so as not to have to look at him as she said: 'Thank you for not mentioning what happened to Aunt Maggie, by the way.'

'Not at all.'

She turned to look at him. 'Would you like some coffee?'

He smiled. 'That's very kind of you. Yes, I would.'

As she took down another cup and saucer she admitted grudgingly to herself that Jean had been right, when he smiled he certainly looked less forbidding— almost handsome in a way. As she put the cup on the tray she was acutely aware of his eyes on her.

'They seem to be progressing well with the conversion,' he remarked. 'This will be a very pleasant place to work in when it's finished.'

'Yes, it will,' Meryl nodded. 'At first there was a little trouble with the planning people, of course—this being a listed building. But Grandfather took care of all that. You have to leave the façade as it is, you know. That's why all the work has to be done at the rear.'

'I realise that. I'm not a complete philistine, you know.' He grinned, obviously enjoying her blush. 'I know that this was your family home too. How do you feel about that side of it?'

She shrugged. 'Grandfather had planned it for so long, I've had plenty of time to get used to the idea.'

He paused, eyeing her thoughtfully. 'Good—so if I were to ask you to move out of this flat, to make room for a caretaker, you'd view the idea sympathetically?'

She spun round to stare at him. 'Leave my flat? But why should I?'

He pulled out a chair from the table and sat down. 'I've been thinking about the security of a place like this since I looked round last night. There's a lot of expensive equipment here—not to mention the valuable and dangerous drugs in the dispensary. It's essential that we engage a caretaker.'

'I don't see why when I live on the premises,' Meryl argued. 'There's a very efficient burglar alarm being fitted too, and you could always employ a security officer if you wanted to.'

His eyebrows rose. 'Thank you, but I'd prefer a resident caretaker,' he said firmly. 'And while we're on the subject, Miss Taylor, there's something I'd like to have straight between us from now on. *I* have been appointed as senior doctor here, so in future *I* will be making the decisions. Do I make myself clear?'

She stood up to face him, her cheeks colouring. 'So in actual fact you're *evicting* me from this flat,' she said hotly. 'The flat my grandfather had converted for me specially?'

His eyes were hard as they stared back into hers. There was a pause, then he said: 'The kettle's threatening to boil over. Are you going to make that cup of coffee?'

Meryl fought down the urge to tell him to go and boil his head as she turned and switched off the kettle, pouring water into the two cups on the tray.

'I hope you don't mind instant,' she mumbled. She had promised Aunt Maggie that she'd try to get along with him, but it wasn't going to be easy—not easy at all!

He took the cup she handed him and helped himself to sugar, stirring thoughtfully. 'Look,' he said at last, glancing up at her, 'we really do have to talk, Meryl—I can call you Meryl, by the way, can't I?'

She shrugged ungraciously. 'I don't suppose I can stop you.'

He ignored the remark. 'Right. Now I know that this has been your family home and it will be a wrench for you to leave it. I'm not entirely unsympathetic, you know. But your aunt has already made the sacrifice. If possible I'd like you to move out this week.'

She took a sip of her boiling coffee, wincing as it scalded her tongue. 'This week! I take it you have something lined up for me? A park bench, perhaps?'

He laughed. 'Now, be reasonable. If you were to take

a job in another town you wouldn't expect to have accommodation provided. In the present circumstances I don't think it would be fair to the other members of the team, do you?'

'Are you actually asking my opinion or just making an observation?' she asked him icily.

He stood up to tower above her, his eyes darkening. 'I was *trying* to appeal to your better nature, but I can see that I'm wasting my time! I've told you—I'd like you to move out of the flat this week if possible, so that the new caretaker can move in as soon as the centre is open. I'm sure you can move in with your aunt until you find a suitable flat.'

She looked up at him, the amber eyes blazing. 'You've already discussed this with her, then?'

'That's right, during our brief meetings we've managed to cover a great deal of ground. Your aunt is a very co-operative woman.' He looked levelly back into the flashing eyes. 'I'd like to make it quite clear that I intend to run the Wellford Centre as efficiently as possible,' he told her. 'With or without your help.' He handed her his empty cup and walked towards the door, stopping as he reached it. 'Oh, by the way, your aunt tells me that some of the new surgery equipment has been delivered. I believe it's locked safely away in one of the completed rooms downstairs and that you have the key. I'd like to have a look at it while I'm here, if you don't mind.'

Without a word Meryl went to the writing desk in the living room and took out the key, holding it out to him. He shook his head.

'I meant I'd like you to come with me—and bring the invoices with you, please, so that we can check them together.'

She sighed exaggeratedly, turning to the drawer to look for the invoices.

'I have to be in Northwich by two-thirty,' she told him tartly as she went towards the door.

He smiled grimly. 'I can assure you I shan't keep you any longer than necessary!'

Without waiting for him Meryl ran swiftly down the stairs, one flight after another, trying hard to contain the anger that boiled inside her. She had tried—she really had! As she neared the bottom she thought she heard him call something out to her and turned to look over her shoulder, and the next moment she cried out in alarm as her foot encountered an empty space instead of the floor. She had completely forgotten the missing boards! To her shocked surprise she found herself wedged waist-high in the void between foundations and floor.

'Oh dear! Don't tell me you're accident-prone!' Gareth's lips twitched as he looked down at her. 'Are you hurt—*again*?'

The only thing that was badly hurt was Meryl's pride as she struggled out of the hole in the floor, ignoring the hand he offered.

'I'm all right, thank you.' Her voice sounded thick as she forced it past the knot of tears in her throat. What a day this was turning out to be! She was halfway out of the hole when two hands grasped her round the waist and heaved her unceremoniously to her feet.

'There—that's better.' He bent to brush the dust from her skirt, then noticed the graze on her shin that was beginning to ooze a few drops of blood. As though she were a small child her took her shoulders and sat her firmly down on the stairs, bending to examine it more closely.

'Mmm, that looks quite nasty—and you've torn your tights too. Look, if you give me the key I'll go and check the equipment while you go upstairs and see to it.'

She pushed him aside and stood up, gritting her teeth as the graze began to sting. 'I'm quite all right—I told you. It was my fault for not looking where I was going. I thought I heard you call something out to me.'

'I did.' He grinned ruefully at her. 'I said "Mind the hole in the floor"!'

Meryl ticked off the items on the invoices while he inspected them and pronounced everything satisfactory. When he had finished she looked pointedly at her watch.

'If you're sure that's all—' He was standing with his back to the door, but he did not move out of the way to allow her to pass. Instead he stood looking down at her.

'I'm sorry we seem to have got off to such a bad start, Meryl,' he said quietly. 'But I'm sure that when you've had time to think about it you'll agree that it would be much better for you to live independently outside the centre. Living 'over the shop', so to speak, is always a mistake, I feel.'

Meryl did not answer but stood tapping her foot as she waited for him to get out of her way. He ignored the pointed gesture and went on:

'As soon as I take up my appointment officially I shall call a meeting. I shall be most interested to hear everyone's ideas.'

Meryl forced back a desire to ask him why, since he seemed to prefer his own. 'Really?' she said. 'I shall begin packing tonight. And now I'm afraid you really will have to excuse me. I have work to attend to.'

He stepped aside and she swept out of the room to limp back up the stairs once out of his sight. Back in the flat she closed the door and leaned against it, pulling a face at her reflection in the hall mirror. *Damn* Gareth Owen-Thomas! He really was a pig—the sort who didn't care whose face he stepped on as long as he got what he wanted. She bent to touch her grazed leg tenderly, then began to peel off her ruined tights. Suddenly she remembered something with a howl of anguish. She had put them on new only this morning. They were her last pair!

CHAPTER THREE

THE combined clinic at Northwich General was so absorbing that Meryl almost forgot her troubles. This afternoon two of the patients being seen had been referred by her and so she had a special interest. The team of experts who observed them from the other side of the one-way mirror were a child psychiatrist, a teacher of the deaf, a consultant neurologist and a plastic surgeon, as well as the head of the physiotherapy department. Before the first of Meryl's patients was seen she explained that although everything possible had been done, including the fitting of an Edinburgh Masker, eight-year-old David continued to stammer. She had come to the conclusion that the trouble might well stem from a deeper cause, and now, during a gentle talk with the psychiatrist's assistant, it emerged that David had a particularly clever elder brother. It seemed that ever since he had first started school he had felt under pressure to do as well, and it could well be this pressure that was causing his speech difficulties. It was decided that he should have further therapy with Meryl, while seeing the psychiatrist at the same time.

The second of her patients was more difficult. Meryl had worked with five-year-old Rachel for several months. The family had come to live in Millington from the North of England when the father had got a job with the construction company engaged on the maintenance of the gas rig and the little girl had been referred by her own GP. Meryl had suspected autism, and now she awaited the reaction of the team. It was decided that the child should be admitted for clinical tests, and Meryl went off to find the mother and explain what would happen.

On her way home Meryl called on a patient who had recently been discharged from hospital. Paul Dixon was a young married man who had been involved in a serious car accident. He had suffered brain damage which had partially paralysed him and temporarily robbed him of his speech. It was Meryl's first visit to him, and she felt a little apprehensive as she rang the front doorbell. Often when patients first came home they were very depressed, and it was her job to assure him and his wife that, given time and patience, he would learn to use his vocal equipment again.

The girl who opened the door to her was about Meryl's own age, but lines of strain and tiredness made her look much older. Meryl smiled as she introduced herself:

'I'm Meryl Taylor, the speech therapist—Mr Forbes, your husband's consultant, may have told you I'd be calling. I was on my way back from Northwich, so I thought I'd pop in.'

The girl nodded. 'Come in. He's in the sitting room.'

'How is he settling down now that he's at home?' Meryl asked.

Mrs Dixon looked close to tears as she replied: 'I don't know how I'm going to cope. He's so cross all the time—I can't seem to do a thing right.' She shook her head despairingly. 'We've only been married eighteen months, you know. Everything was so wonderful, until —until this happened. Now—' She broke off, biting her lip. 'Oh dear, I feel so disloyal. I'm sure you haven't come here to listen to my troubles, have you?'

Meryl laid a hand on her arm. 'That's just what I am here for. It's best if I hear about any problems you're having so that I can try to help you with them. This is always a difficult time, you know. You're not the only one who feels as you do. I'd hazard a guess that at the moment he's feeling very frustrated and inadequate, that's why he's so cross.'

She smiled reassuringly, taking her notes out of her briefcase and looking at them. 'I see that your husband is making excellent progress with the physiotherapy and the doctor's report is most encouraging. The prognosis is very promising.' She smiled. 'Let's go in and see him, shall we?'

Paul Dixon sat in his wheelchair by the fireplace. In front of him was a small table on which was a half-completed jigsaw puzzle. He was a tall, good-looking young man of about twenty-six, with dark wavy hair and expressive brown eyes, but Meryl noticed that his left hand lay limply on his knee. His wife introduced Meryl, an over-bright smile on her face and two spots of colour in her cheeks:

'This is Miss Taylor, Paul. She's the speech therapist that Mr Forbes told us would be calling to see you.'

The young man managed a weak smile and Meryl sat down opposite him.

'Please try not to worry too much about your voice, Mr Dixon,' she said. 'I daresay Mr Forbes will have explained to you that at present you're suffering from something known as dysarthia. You know exactly what you want to say, but the sounds that come out don't seem to be related to it at all.' She smiled sympathetically. 'It must be very frustrating for you, but it will get better, I promise you. It's rather like trying to find your way out of a maze, but there *is* a way, and with my help you'll soon find it.' She smiled at Paul's wife, who was hovering close to her husband's side. 'Now, as you probably know, our new health centre is to be opened soon, which means that you'll be able to attend the clinic here in Millington instead of having to go all the way to Northwich every week. If you don't have transport that can be laid on for you. As soon as I know the date and time of the first clinic I'll let you know, and in the meantime I'll come and see you here at home, if that's all right.' She put her notes away in her briefcase and rose to go, but Mrs Dixon said quickly:

'Oh, please, you will stay and have a cup of tea with us, won't you? I was just going to make a cup.'

Meryl was about to refuse when she suddenly noticed the look of mute appeal on Paul's face and said:

'Well, that's very kind of you. I must admit that I could do with a cup.'

The girl looked pleased. 'By the way, I'm Julie,' she said from the doorway. 'I'm sure we'd both like you to call us by our Christian names—especially as it looks as though we'll be seeing a lot of each other over the coming months.'

'I agree. I'm Meryl—please call me that too.'

When the door had closed Meryl leaned forward to pick up a piece of Paul's puzzle. 'There,' she said, snapping it into place, 'I've been dying to do that ever since I came into the room.' But when she looked at the young man she saw that he was indicating a pad and pencil, just out of his reach on the table. 'Oh, do you want this?' She pushed it towards him.

He seized it gratefully and began to scribble, passing it to her after a few moments. She read: 'She fusses so—treats me like a backward child.'

Meryl smiled at him as she tore off the page and pushed it into her pocket. 'It's only natural. It's hard for her too, you know,' she told him quietly. 'She's only trying to do her best for you.' She reached out to touch his hand. 'Try to go along with it for now, Paul,' she advised. 'Don't expect too much too soon and you'll be all right.'

Meryl arrived back at Wellford House just as evening surgery was beginning. She put her head round the door of the reception office.

'Would you ask Dr Taylor to look in on me before she goes home, please, Sandra?' she asked the receptionist.

Upstairs in the flat she went through to the bedroom and began to pack. The sooner she got out, the better, though where she would find a flat she hadn't the least idea. Since the town had begun to expand it had been all but impossible to find rented accommodation; everything available was occupied, with newcomers waiting for new houses to be built for them.

When she had done as much as she could she went through to the kitchen and made herself a sandwich. She wasn't hungry enough to want to cook; the thought of leaving the only home of her own she had ever known had quite taken her appetite away. She had just finished eating when there was a tap on the door and her aunt walked in.

'Hello, dear. I've just finished surgery. Sandra said you wanted to see me.'

Meryl got up from the table and went across to put on

the kettle for coffee. 'That's right. I had a visit from Dr Owen-Thomas at lunchtime. He didn't wait for our appointment but came up here to see me instead.' She turned to look at her aunt. 'He tells me that you and he have decided I should be evicted from this flat.'

Dr Margaret sighed and sat down at the table. 'Oh dear, what a very emotive way of putting it! I did tell him I would speak to you about that.'

'You didn't mention it this morning, though, did you?' Meryl said accusingly. 'It would have been nicer to have heard it from you instead of from a complete stranger. Dr Owen-Thomas also told me that you've offered to put me up until I can find another flat,' she went on. 'Would you mind if I moved in with you as soon as possible? Staying on here now is only prolonging the agony, and anyway, I understand you've already adver-tised for a caretaker!'

Margaret sighed. 'I do wish you wouldn't be so dra-matic about it all, Meryl. And I wish you wouldn't speak of Gareth as though he were some kind of arch-villain. I know there've been misunderstandings, but he's really a very nice person, you know.'

'So you keep telling me,' Meryl said sharply. 'Perhaps one day I shall be lucky enough to be able to see him as you do. So far he's done nothing to endear him to me at all!'

Margaret got to her feet decisively. 'Why don't you come home with me right now? We really need to talk, and as far as I can see you haven't eaten properly. Libby has one of her casseroles on the go and there'll be plenty for you too.'

Meryl opened her mouth to refuse, then closed it again and sat down at the table with a sigh, realising for the first time how very tired she was.

'Oh well, perhaps I will. I've had a pretty heavy day, what with one thing and another.'

'Good! That's settled, then.' Margaret looked down at Meryl's leg, and noticed the graze on it. 'What have you been doing to yourself?'

'Falling down a hole in the floor—thanks to your beloved Gareth,' Meryl said wryly. 'But it's a long story. Maybe we'd better have that meal before I start telling it to you!'

Woodbine Cottage stood at the centre of what had been the old village. It now stood on the outskirts of the new town of Millington. It had everything that Margaret had always wanted—a thatched roof, a walled garden with delphiniums and hollyhocks and its own path leading down to what was still an unspoiled part of the beach. She had bought it soon after her father's death and moved in, taking Libby, the housekeeper who had been with the family for longer than Meryl could remember.

Margaret opened the front door and called out as she took off her coat:

'Coo-ee, Libby! I'm home—and I've brought a surprise for you!'

The housekeeper came out into the hall wiping her hands on the blue striped apron she wore. She was short and comfortably plump, with white frizzy hair and bright blue eyes. When she saw Meryl her round face broke into a smile.

'Well, well—and about time too! We've hardly seen anything of you at all since we moved in here.'

'It looks as though I'll be making up for lost time from now on,' Meryl said wryly.

'There's enough dinner for two, isn't there, Libby?' Margaret broke in hastily. 'And Meryl will be staying the night.'

The housekeeper beamed. 'Of course there's enough. And the bed is made up in the spare room. I'll just slip up and switch on the electric blanket to make sure it's aired.'

Margaret opened the door of the living room, smiling at Meryl. 'She'll be just like a mother hen with one chick! You know how she loves to have you about the place. Only natural, I suppose, seeing that she practically brought you up.' She crossed the room to a small cocktail cabinet, turning to her niece enquiringly. 'Will you have a sherry before your dinner?'

Meryl nodded and sank into the deep settee. 'You'd better not make me too comfortable. I don't intend to stay here any longer than necessary, Aunt Maggie. We both like our independence too much to think of living in the same house for good. Though where I'm going to find a flat I don't know.'

Margaret handed her a glass of sherry and sat down in the chair opposite.

'I've been thinking about that,' she said thoughtfully. 'There's always the beach house. The season is over now and we hardly ever use it any more anyway. I was thinking of selling it, but it could come in useful. Would you like to move in there for the time being?'

Meryl's face brightened. 'What a good idea! But it is a little on the large side for one person, don't you think?'

Margaret waved a hand dismissively. 'I shouldn't worry about that, I'm sure there'll be someone who'll be willing to share with you later.'

The beach house was a chalet-type building that the

Taylor family had owned since Meryl was a small child. When she was younger they had often used it at weekends and sometimes let it to friends and relatives for holidays in the summer months. It stood on a grassy plateau about thirty feet above the beach, and as a child Meryl had loved spending weekends there, running with her bucket and spade down the rickety wooden steps to play on the soft golden sand. She had very happy memories of the place.

'I was thinking of enquiring about one of those new studio flats they're building for single people on the new estate,' she told her aunt. 'But it'll be some time before they're ready. I might even get you to let the beach house to me on a permanent basis.' She looked at Margaret, but her aunt looked thoughtful.

'Let's just see how things go first,' she said. She looked at Meryl. 'You're not too unhappy about leaving the flat at Wellford House, are you, dear?' she asked. 'Now that it's to be a health centre it really wouldn't be practical for you to go on living there. You do see that, don't you?'

Meryl sighed. 'I'm beginning to get used to the idea —though I still think it would have been better coming from you.'

'Was Gareth actually unkind to you over it?' asked Margaret, frowning. 'Did he tell you in an abrupt way?'

'No—it's just that I think he might have left it to you.' Meryl frowned. 'He's rather an insensitive man, isn't he? Unimaginative.'

Margaret smiled. 'I'm sure he isn't really. Forgive me, Meryl, but perhaps he thought he should put you in your place after the things he overheard you saying about him the other evening!'

Meryl snorted angrily and was about to make a

remark when the door opened and Libby looked in to tell them that dinner was ready.

Later, when she was in bed, reading, there was a tap on the door. She looked up.

'Come in.'

The door opened to admit Libby. She wore her cosy red wool dressing gown and her hair was in rollers, covered by a hairnet. She carried a tray on which was a glass of milk and a plate of biscuits. Meryl smiled, putting down her book.

'Oh, Libby, you really shouldn't spoil me like this.'

The housekeeper smiled. 'I know how you've always liked your bedtime drink, and I don't often get the chance to spoil you nowadays, do I? Not since you've become such an independent young woman.' She sat down on the edge of the bed. 'If you ask me, I think it's a shame, you having to move out of the lovely little flat your granddad had made for you. What are you going to do?'

'It's all arranged. I'm going to have the beach house temporarily, until I can find somewhere else,' Meryl told her as she sipped her milk. 'Maybe I'll even rent it permanently and do it up a bit.'

Libby looked doubtful. 'Well, it might be all right for now, but I doubt if you'll be warm enough once the winter sets in. There's no central heating there, you know.' She shook her head at Meryl. 'What you need is a nice husband.'

Meryl laughed. 'Oh, do I?'

Libby smiled dreamily. 'Just think—a cosy little house with all your own things round you—hubby coming home at the end of the day—maybe even a baby or two. Wouldn't that be nice?'

'But I like my life as it is,' Meryl protested. 'I have a job I love and I can please myself. Besides—' she pulled a face, 'I've got a horrible suspicion that all that domesticity would get boring after a while.'

Libby sighed wistfully. 'Well, I don't know about that. I never had the chance to find out, did I?' Libby had come to the Taylor household as a young widow, just after her husband had died after only a few months of marriage. Meryl leaned forward to hug her.

'Oh, I'm sorry, Libby, I forgot. How thoughtless of me!'

'Don't you fret about that. It was all a long time ago,' the housekeeper assured her. 'I do hope you're not going to take after your Aunt Maggie, though. I always hoped she'd marry, but it wasn't to be. Sometimes I think she regrets it now, between you and me.' She pushed the plate of biscuits towards Meryl. 'Go on girl, have another. You're as thin as a rake!' She watched with satisfaction as Meryl took another biscuit and munched it. 'What do you think of the new doctor, then?' she asked suddenly. Meryl pulled a face.

'Do you want to put me off my milk and biscuits?'

Libby grinned. 'He's very handsome—rugged, we'd have called him in my day. A real *man*.'

'Mmm, some might call him that, I suppose. *I'd* call him brusque and insensitive, personally,' Meryl said with feeling. 'I can't think why he was appointed.'

Libby shrugged. 'I'm sure they knew what they were doing. He's very well suited for the job,' she said. 'And of course, with your aunt knowing his father—'

'She *what*?' Meryl sat up straight, staring at the housekeeper. 'Well! I'd never have thought her capable of nepotism!'

'Oh, it's nothing like that, I'm sure,' Libby assured her hastily. 'And it wasn't entirely up to her anyway, was it? It's a long time since she last saw him.' She looked at Meryl. 'All I meant was that it helps to know a bit about a person's background, that's all.'

'I can't see that that has anything to do with it at all!' Meryl said hotly. 'A man is what he makes of himself. I don't see why he should have labels hung round his neck because of his background.'

Next morning at breakfast she taxed her aunt with it. 'Is it true that you once knew Dr Owen-Thomas's father?'

Margaret looked up sharply. 'Who told you that?'

'Libby happened to let it slip. She obviously thought I knew.'

'It's sheer coincidence—and *knew* is the operative word,' Margaret told her. 'It was years ago, when I was at Cambridge. Gareth's father was an engineering student at the time. I'd forgotten all about him. It was the name that rang a bell.' She looked at her niece. 'But it certainly had nothing to do with Gareth's getting the appointment, if that's what you're implying.'

'I should hope not indeed!' Meryl admonished.

By the end of the week Meryl had moved all her things to the beach house. Each evening when she had finished work she drove over with another suitcase full, until by Friday evening the flat was completely cleared. She stood in the middle of the living room, looking around her for the last time. It would be strange, living at the beach house—knowing that she would never be coming back here again. The furniture was not her own and was to be left for the caretaker who would be moving in, but already the place looked bare and impersonal without her small possessions and photographs scattered about. She closed the door with a resigned sigh and clattered down the bare stairs. The new carpets were to be laid on Monday morning and the following week the health centre would be officially opened. It was something she had been looking forward to—until the advent of Dr Owen-Thomas.

There were three bedrooms at the beach house, and Meryl chose the one upstairs with its view of the sea. She made up the bed with her own duvet, unpacked the last of her cases and put her things away in the wardrobe. It was a beautiful evening, warm and mellow. She stood looking out of the window, across the stretch of grass to the sea beyond. It was mirror-smooth, something one rarely saw on this coast, and she was suddenly seized by the urge to go for a swim. This Indian summer weather couldn't last; in another few weeks it would be winter. On this coast it could change overnight, so this might well be her last chance this year. She began to pull off her clothes, suddenly quite excited at the prospect. A few minutes later she was running across the grass in her white bikini, towel in hand, pattering barefoot down the wooden steps on to the sunwarmed sand.

She swam for a while, then turned on to her back and let the gentle swell rock her lazily. The water was deliciously soft and silky. It was a wonderful feeling. Perhaps living at the beach house would be fun, she told herself as she floated with her eyes closed against the glare of the evening sun. It was true that there was no central heating, but the living room had a large open fireplace. She imagined herself getting up early to collect driftwood from the beach—sitting in front of a roaring wood fire on winter evenings, snug and secure against the howling of the sea and wind outside.

At last she turned and swam ashore. The sun had gone by the time she reached the beach, leaving the sea a dull green. The sand was cold under her feet and she wrapped herself in her towel, her teeth chattering slightly as she ran back up the steps and across to the house. In the ground floor bathroom she turned on the shower and peeled off her bikini to step in. The hot water soon made her skin glow and she sang as she shampooed her hair. Stepping out of the shower, she wrapped a towel round herself and tucked it in, sarong fashion, while she rubbed her hair vigorously, then she went through to the kitchen in search of something to eat.

In the doorway she stopped dead. The bag of food she had shopped for on her way here and left on the table had been rifled and someone had made themself a hasty snack—the telltale crumbs of bread and cheese were scattered on the table to prove it. Not only that, but the kettle had been filled and plugged in. She turned quickly and almost ran straight into the arms of a man standing in the doorway.

'Oh! What are you doing here?'

Gareth Owen-Thomas was eyeing her with frank appreciation, a smile on his lips. 'Moving in, as a matter of fact,' he told her casually.

Meryl grasped at the slipping towel, suddenly aware of her near-nakedness.

'Not if I can help it!' she told him, her cheeks crimson.

'I can assure you that it's only temporary,' he told her. 'I got back from Wales this afternoon—all set to move into the hotel I'd booked before I left. But it seems that the idiot who took the booking was looking at the wrong week. This week the place is full up—some kind of conference going on, it seems.' He shrugged. 'I threw myself on your aunt's mercy, but she has the decorators in, so she gave me the key to this place.' He smiled. 'She did mention that there was another tenant here, but she seemed to think you wouldn't mind.'

'Oh—well, we'll see about that!' Almost speechless with rage, Meryl pointed to the bag on the table. 'That happens to be my supper you've been helping yourself to!'

He grinned apologetically. 'Sorry. I'm afraid I couldn't resist making myself a sandwich. I haven't had anything to eat since breakfast. It's a long drive from Wales, you know.'

'Excuse me!' Meryl strode out of the kitchen, through to the living room where she shut the door firmly behind her. Picking up the telephone, she dialled her aunt's number.

'Hello, Dr Margaret Taylor here. Can I help you?'

'You certainly can! What's this man doing at the beach house?' Meryl demanded.

'Oh, Meryl, it's you. I tried to ring you earlier, but I couldn't get any reply. The poor man simply hasn't anywhere else to go. I was sure you wouldn't mind. After all, there's plenty of room. You need hardly come into contact with him at all if you don't want to.'

'That's hardly the point. Can I come back there?' asked Meryl.

'I'm sorry, dear, the decorators started work on the spare room this morning. I could have put Gareth up myself otherwise.'

'What about the Taggarts? He stayed with them last time.'

'That's out too, I'm afraid. Mike's brother and his family are over from Canada on a visit. They arrive tomorrow.'

Meryl sighed. 'Honestly, Aunt Maggie, it just isn't on. What will people think?'

Her aunt sounded surprised. 'Think? What *should* they think? Plenty of flats and houses have mixed tenants sharing nowadays. Anyway, I don't see why anyone should know unless you choose to tell them.'

Meryl saw she was in a cleft stick situation; she appeared to be stuck with Dr Owen-Thomas whether she liked it or not. She stared speechlessly into the receiver until she heard her aunt clear her throat at the other end of the line.

'Is that all, then, dear?' she asked. 'Libby has dinner on the table, and you know how cross she gets if you leave it till it's cold.'

Meryl said goodbye and hung up. As she walked out into the hall again she shivered and suddenly remembered her state of undress. She was about to go upstairs when Gareth appeared in the kitchen doorway.

'Is there anywhere I can leave my car?' he asked.

Meryl sighed resignedly. 'There's a garage at the end of the track. My car's in there, but I think you'll find room,' she told him. 'And now if you'll excuse me I'll go and put some clothes on.'

He grinned at her. 'Please don't go to any trouble just for me!'

Meryl coloured. 'I'm not in the habit of walking round like this. I've been swimming, as it happens.'

He shrugged. 'No need to make excuses. I'm all for it, personally.' He saw her colour and reached out to cover the hand that lay on the banister rail. 'Please—I'm only teasing. And I'm sorry about pinching your food. Perhaps you'll let me take you out to dinner to make up for it?'

She shook her head. 'No, thank you. I'm sure there'll be enough left. I'm not very hungry now anyway!' And with this ungracious remark she walked up the stairs and firmly closed the door of her room.

She climbed into her underwear and pulled on a pair of jeans and a sweater. Her hair had almost dried now and fell to her shoulders in soft waves, and as she sat down at the dressing table the gentle evening light burnished it to a rich copper. Quite deliberately she took out a thin ribbon and tied it tightly back. The swim had made her skin glow and her eyes were shining, more green than amber this evening with the anger she felt. She automatically picked up her lipstick, then threw it down again. No need to make herself attractive for that man! The last thing she wanted to do was to create the impression that she was trying to please him.

In the doorway of the kitchen she stopped short for the second time that evening. The table was set with a red checked cloth, in the centre of which burned a single candle in an empty Chianti bottle. Two places were laid and Gareth was just turning from the stove, a steaming plate in either hand.

'Spanish omelettes,' he announced. 'Rather a speciality of mine. I hope you like them. And I hope you'll forgive me for helping myself to your food again. I promise I'll replace it tomorrow.' He put the plates on the table and pulled out her chair with a flourish, a tea-towel draped over one arm. 'Will Madame be seated?'

Disarmed, Meryl sat down and looked at her plate.

The omelette smelled delicious, and she suddenly realised how hungry her swim had made her.

'Thank you,' she said. 'You really shouldn't have gone to so much trouble.'

'I'm used to cooking for myself, being a bachelor,' he said, handing her a plate of bread and butter. 'I really am sorry about intruding on your privacy. I'm sure we shall be able to work out a plan that will keep us out of each other's way. And it's only until I find myself a suitable house or flat.'

'That could take time,' Meryl told him. 'The town was never meant to hold so many people. The population has outgrown the accommodation and until the building programme gets under way—'

'Well, maybe I'll be lucky,' he interrupted. 'Anyway, I promise to do my best to be out from under your feet as soon as I can.'

As they ate Gareth asked her about her family, and Meryl soon found the warm food and drink relaxing her. She found herself telling him about her childhood at Wellford House.

'My parents were killed in a plane crash when I was six. They were on their way home from a holiday in Italy—the first they'd had for years. It was a second honeymoon and I was staying with Aunt Maggie and Grandfather at the time. I just stayed on.'

He looked sympathetic. 'How dreadful for you. You must have been very lonely.'

She shook her head. 'Not really. Of course Granddad and Aunt Maggie were always busy, but Libby spent a lot of time with me. She's still housekeeper at Woodbine Cottage, I daresay you've met her. She came to work for Grandfather as a young woman, just after her husband died. I suppose looking back, I made up for the children she'd never had. It was a very happy childhood really.'

'And you decided to follow the family tradition and go in for medicine?' he asked.

'No. To begin with I had my heart set on a career in the theatre,' she told him.

He stopped eating to look at her in surprise. 'An actress?' The idea seemed to amuse him. 'What went wrong? Now that I think of it, I'd have thought you were ideally cut out for that kind of work.'

Meryl frowned, not sure whether he was complimenting her or not. 'Perhaps, like most people, you have the wrong idea about what makes a good actress,' she remarked.

He shrugged. 'I do know that one needs looks. And nature certainly wasn't in a stingy mood when she handed you your share.'

Meryl blushed hotly. 'Be that as it may, I was wrong. I just didn't have the necessary talent. It was only then that I realised that I'd chosen the stage as a kind of protest. Everyone expected me to go into medicine, you see, and I've always hated having my mind made up for me.'

He grinned. 'I can imagine. So what happened next?'

Meryl poured out more coffee. 'I had to come home and admit to Granddad that I'd made a mistake— wasted his money. But as usual he took it all very calmly. He had the perfect practical solution—he suggested that I try speech therapy. It was a wonderful idea. I even found I could train at the same college. All I had to do was to switch courses. I didn't even have to lose touch with my friends.'

'Or lose face either,' Gareth remarked perceptively.

Meryl's chin went up as she rose from the table and began to clear away the dishes. 'It must be wonderful to be so clever,' she said sarcastically. 'On the other hand, I imagine it could get you into trouble too.'

He ignored the jibe and rose to help her with the washing-up. For a few minutes they worked in silence, then he asked:

'By the way, does any of the bedrooms have a telephone extension?'

She nodded. 'Yes, the one upstairs—mine.'

'I see.' He dried a plate reflectively. 'I think perhaps I'd better have that one, then, don't you? Because of the nights when I'll be on call.'

Meryl's eyebrows rose. 'I really don't see why you should. I've moved all my things in now. And it isn't as if it's the only telephone in the house. If you're on call and you have to get up anyhow, it won't hurt you to get up and answer the telephone, will it?'

'I happen to be a very heavy sleeper,' he told her. 'I may not hear it ringing.'

She smiled at him smugly. 'Then I shall have to get up and knock on your door, shan't I?'

'Won't that be rather inconvenient for you?'

'Not at all. I'd rather do that than move out, and as you said yourself, it *is* only temporary.' She glared at him. 'I was here first, remember—and it was you who had me evicted from my flat!'

He shook his head sadly. 'Oh dear, just when I was beginning to tell myself that you weren't a spoilt brat after all! Over supper you very nearly convinced me that all that arrogance was simply due to a rather unfortunate manner.'

Meryl threw down the tea-cloth, her cheeks flaming.

'You can insult me as much as you like, but you are *not* having my room!' she told him firmly.

She began to put away the dishes, clattering them angrily, while Gareth stood watching her with an enigmatic expression. At last he said:

'Look, Meryl, if we're going to share this place I think we should make some kind of effort to get along—be friends.' She did not reply and after a moment he added: 'Please, will you stop all that bad-tempered banging about and listen to me for a moment?'

Something in his tone made her stop and turn to look at him, and to her surprise she saw controlled anger burning in his eyes. It had a calming effect on her. So she was getting to him after all! Very slowly and deliberately she closed the cupboard door and folded the damp tea-cloth.

'I must remember to buy some new rubber gloves,' she said half to herself. She looked at him. 'As for being "friends", as you put it, I'd rather—' She bit her lip and took a step backwards, feeling the edge of the sink unit pressing into her back. Had she gone too far? She'd heard somewhere that these Celtic types could be quite violent when roused. At the moment he looked positively dangerous as he towered over her.

'Go on,' he challenged. 'You'd rather what?'

She began to turn away, but suddenly his hands shot out. He grasped her shoulders, his fingers hard as steel. Her head snapped back to look up at him, a protest on her lips, but before she could utter it his lips came down on hers in a kiss that dashed the breath from her body. As he released her she stared wordlessly up at him, stunned into silence. He looked down into her eyes and she saw that the anger in them had softened. The iron grip on her shoulders relaxed a little.

'Sorry—it was the only way I could stop you from saying something you might have regretted,' he offered. 'Where did you get such a vitriolic tongue, Meryl Taylor?'

'I don't know—I didn't know I had one till I met you,' she told him breathlessly.

Suddenly he smiled. 'Well, at least I know how to stop it now, don't I?' he asked, his grey eyes twinkling.

CHAPTER FOUR

ANYONE overhearing the speech therapy session at St Winifred's School for the handicapped that sunny autumn morning could have been forgiven for thinking that a party was in full swing. Meryl was taking a group of advanced ten-year-olds and they were enjoying their favourite game of Twenty Questions. She had promised they should finish the session with this as they had done so well in their morning's work. As they played, the children calling out their questions excitedly as they drew nearer to the solution, Mrs Venables, the headmistress, slipped into the room and stood quietly at the back. When at last the bell went and the children reluctantly filed out for lunch she smiled at Meryl.

'They do so well with you. You know, one or two of them have improved more since you've been working with them than they have in their whole time at the school.'

Meryl smiled. It was encouragement like this that made her job so rewarding. 'I try not to let them realise it's more than play,' she said as she gathered her things together. 'Children work much better when they're relaxed.'

Mrs Venables saw her looking at her watch. 'I won't keep you,' she said quickly. 'I know it's a big day for you—the official opening of the Wellford Centre. You'll be wanting to run off and get ready. I only wanted to have a quick word with you about a new child who'll be starting with us next week. I thought I should prepare the ground a little. You'll be getting the notes, of course, but I've met him, so I have more first-hand knowledege of the case. In my opinion he doesn't belong in a school of this kind. He's been proved to be above average intelligence, but for the past two years his speech has deteriorated severely. It was thought that a spell here might help, though I have reservations. I do think you might be able to help him, though.'

'Thanks for the vote of confidence.' Meryl smiled as she zipped her briefcase. 'I take it he's dyslalic?'

Mrs Venables nodded. 'And immature for a seven-year-old too, though, as I said before, he's really very bright. Dr Williams, the psychologist at Northwich, sent me some drawings Peter did. I thought you might like to take them away and study them.' She handed Meryl an envelope which she pushed into her briefcase.

'Thanks, they could be interesting and useful. I'll take a look at them later. See you next week, Mrs Venables.'

'Goodbye, dear. Have a good time at the opening. I shall be looking out for a glimpse of you on television this evening!'

Meryl glanced once more at her watch as she ran to the car park. She would have her work cut out now to dash back to the beach house, shower and change into her new dress and be at Wellford House for one o'clock. She unlocked the car and jumped in, switching on and revving the engine anxiously.

As she drove to the beach house she wondered if Gareth had already left for the Centre. Since he had taken up his appointment he had been sharing the old accommodation at Wellford House, using Richard's room on a turn-and-turn-about basis.

Since the evening when he had kissed her she had hardly set eyes on him. Obviously he had been busy, but she felt there was more to it than that. Did he regret his hasty action? He wasn't the type to let it embarrass him. What had happened had clearly been on impulse. Later she had been furious with herself for not reacting more positively to it. She should have slapped his face. He had treated her like some sort of *object.* How dared he think he could sweep her off her feet like some naïve Victorian schoolgirl? Stun her by the sheer force of his male personality?

The dreadful thing was that he had done just that! Never in her entire life would she be able to forgive herself for letting him get away with it. She had stood there, staring up at him like a complete idiot, for what seemed ages, then she had turned and fled to her room, securely bolting the door, her cheeks burning and her heart thudding in her chest. She must have sat staring at her reflection in the dressing table mirror for five whole minutes, trying to sort out the tangle of emotions that churned inside her. It was only later, when she realised what a fool she must have looked, that she had tried to put it right, and by then it had been too late. Gareth was in his own room, unpacking, she could hear him humming tunelessly to himself—he had been right about not being able to sing for toffee! Later he had seemed preoccupied, and she realised it would be impossible to bring up the subject again without making it look as though she wanted to remind him of it!

At the beach house she was relieved to find she had the place to herself. She showered hastily and put on the new grey wool dress, turning to survey herself in the mirror. Yes, it was just the thing for this occasion; plain without being dowdy, smart without being overdressed. She tied a soft scarf of rich violet blue into the neck and combed her hair, catching it back behind her ears with two combs. A pale coral lipstick and a touch of violet eye-shadow emphasised her colouring, and the outfit was finished off by the amethyst earrings her grandfather and Aunt Maggie had given her for her twenty-first birthday. At last, satisfied that she looked her best, she glanced at her watch once more and whisked out of the house to jump back into the car and head for Wellford House. She had made it with minutes to spare. She was slightly surprised when she arrived to see the TV vans outside, and in the entrance hall there seemed to be several dozen men in headphones. The place was festooned with cables, and she picked her way among them, looking for Aunt Maggie. She found her in the large waiting area towards the rear of the building, where the opening ceremony was to be performed. On the wall was the plaque that would later be unveiled by the local MP, Maurice Dunster. Margaret Taylor was peering anxiously under the velvet cloth that covered it.

'Hello, dear. You got here all right, then?' she said abstractedly. 'Oh dear, I do hope this cord doesn't stick. It would be so awful with a TV camera looking on. Somehow it would be such a bad omen.'

Behind them someone laughed. 'There's something very Freudian about Maggie's preoccupation with cords! I wonder if it has anything to do with her work in obstetrics!'

Meryl turned to see Dr Mike Taggart standing behind her, his blue eyes dancing. He stepped forward and grasped Margaret by the waist, turning her round and kissing her soundly on the cheek.

'Will you stop worrying, Dr Taylor!' he demanded in his soft Irish lilt. 'Don't you know that the whole thing will be filmed? If anything goes wrong they can cut and do it again. Sure, isn't that the beauty of TV?' He turned to Meryl 'You know, I wouldn't put it past her not to have checked on the food! This aunt of yours has a very unfeminine mind sometimes.'

Meryl frowned at him. 'If I may say so, Mike, that's an extremely sexist remark!'

He laughed his loud laugh, but Aunt Maggie had clapped a hand to her mouth. 'Sexist it might be—true, it *is*!' And she rushed off in the direction of the meeting room where the buffet lunch was to be eaten.

Mike grinned goodnaturedly at Meryl. 'It's all right, as it happens,' he confided. 'The caterers have been hard at it for the last hour, so they must be about finished by now.' He patted her shoulder. 'Well, how do you feel? A proud day, eh?'

Meryl nodded. For the first time she was beginning to feel a twinge of nerves. Her grandfather would have been so happy to see his dream coming true. Nothing must happen to spoil it.

'If only Granddad could have been here,' she whispered, swallowing hard.

Mike slipped his arm around her shoulders and gave her a hug. 'Maybe he is, love, maybe he is. But however you look at it, it's his day—his little bit of immortality.' He nodded his head towards the plaque on the wall, and Meryl nodded too, smiling up at him.

'I still say you should have put in for the job of senior doctor, Mike,' she told him. 'Why didn't you want it? You've been here longer than any of us, except Aunt Maggie.'

He shrugged. 'Ah, you know as well as I do that I'm best where I am. I'm no good at the organising side of things. Better with people.'

In her heart Meryl knew that he was right. All the patients loved big soft-hearted Dr Taggart. He always had a pocketful of sweets for the children and a cheery smile and a joke for the old folks, but when it came to filling up forms or being organised—it was a good job he had an efficient wife, as he would be the first to own.

At that moment Richard arrived, looking smart in his new grey suit, and Mike gave a low whistle.

'Well, aren't you the dandy!'

Richard coloured. 'It isn't too much, is it?' He looked anxiously at Meryl, who shook her head.

'Of course it isn't. You look very nice. Mike's only trying to draw attention away from the fact that he's the only one who didn't buy a new suit for the occasion.'

Mike pulled a face. 'Jean will tell you how much I hate new clothes. It would have spoiled the day for me, and you wouldn't want that, now would you?' He grinned at them disarmingly. 'And you have to admit that I look a picture.'

'Has the chief arrived yet?' asked Richard, looking at his watch.

Mike nodded. 'He went out to the car park to see if the VIP had arrived,' he told them. 'I have a feeling that he's as nervous as the rest of us.'

The door opened at that moment and as though right on cue Gareth walked in with a tall, distinguished-looking grey-haired man. He introduced him as the Right Honourable Maurice Dunster, MP. They all shook hands with him, then Gareth invited him along to his office to relax with a drink while they awaited the arrival of the Mayor and various other civic dignitaries.

An hour later it was all over, the speeches, the unveiling—which went smoothly in spite of Margaret's fears—and the ceremonial drinking of champagne. Now they were all in the meeting room, enjoying the excellent buffet lunch. Meryl looked around her. Aunt Maggie looked less anxious now that it was all over. She was talking animatedly to Maurice Dunster, and Meryl thought how nice she looked in her navy suit with the froth of lace at the neck and wrists. It was hard to understand why she had never married. She must have been a stunningly beautiful woman in her youth. In her way she still was.

'Well, how did you think it went?'

The voice behind her broke through her reverie and she turned to find herself looking up at Gareth. 'Oh, very well, I think.'

He grinned. 'Are you going to watch it on TV this evening?'

Meryl pulled a face. 'I don't know if I dare. They say it's quite a shock, seeing oneself for the first time.'

He nodded. 'What was that Robbie Burns said about seeing ourselves as others see us?'

'Hello, what's this—a Welshman quoting Burns?' Mike Taggart took Gareth's arm. 'I want you to come and meet old Dr Henderson.' He leaned across to Meryl with a grin and whispered: 'This is something I found myself completely unable to resist—an Irishman, a Scotsman and a Welshman—the oldest joke in the book!' He went off with Gareth, leaving his wife Jean with Meryl. She laughed.

'And we all know how Mike likes old jokes, don't we?'

Meryl sipped her champagne. 'I must say it will be a

relief to all of us when today is over and we can begin working here properly. The last few months have been a bit nerve-racking.'

Jean nodded. 'I agree. By the way, I'm thrilled with my new room. Yours is super too. You are lucky, you know, not many speech therapists are as well equipped —or get to choose all their own things.'

Meryl coloured. 'Don't *you* start rubbing in how spoilt I am!'

Jean looked at her sharply. 'I didn't mean it like that. Has someone been implying that you are?'

Meryl sighed. 'No, of course they haven't. Take no notice, my nerves are a bit frayed, that's all.'

Jean took her arm. 'Come and meet the Centre's new nurse, Sister Jane Pritchard. Your aunt tells me you and she haven't met yet.'

'No, she was appointed the same weekend as Dr Owen-Thomas—the weekend that I was away,' Meryl told her.

'There she is, over there.' Jean pointed to a group of people on the other side of the room. 'She's the pretty blonde in the black dress.'

Meryl stared hard. 'Oh, is *that* her? I've been wondering who she was.'

Jean grinned. 'Glamorous, isn't she? Gareth seems to think so too. I've been watching him, and he can hardly take his eyes off her. Anyway, come and say hello.' She took Meryl's arm and propelled her across the room, introducing her. A moment later Gareth joined them.

'So Jean has introduced you. I was just about to come and do it myself.' He smiled at both girls, then dropped an arm casually across Jane's shoulders, looking down at her solicitously.

'Tell me, have you managed to find anywhere to live yet?'

She shook her head. 'I'm still in the same digs. But I can't grumble—they're very good as digs go, but rather claustrophobic. The landlady is the sort that likes to mother one.'

Gareth grinned. 'I know what you mean.' He gave Meryl the ghost of a wink. 'That's one problem I don't have at the moment, though.' He looked back into the large blue eyes of Sister Jane Pritchard. 'Are you doing anything this evening?' She shook her head, the blonde curls dancing. He smiled. 'Good, have dinner with me, then?' he looked quickly at Meryl. 'Oh, you too, Meryl, if you're free, of course.'

'Oh, but I'm not!' she told him quickly. The last thing she needed was to be patronised by Dr Owen-Thomas! 'I'm going out with Richard, aren't I, darling?' She grabbed Richard's arm as he was passing. He locked surprised.

'What's that?'

'Dinner—this evening. You asked me ages ago, remember?'

He stared at her, then winced as she gave his ankle a sly kick. 'Oh!—oh, yes, of course—dinner. I'll come out to the beach house and pick you up at about seven, shall I?'

'Yes—oh *no*!' Meryl coloured as she remembered that Richard still didn't know about her 'tenant'. 'I'll drive in to you. I mean, it's silly, isn't it, coming all the way out to the beach house only to come back again?'

Gareth looked at Richard. 'If you've got a minute, Dr Jessel, I'd like to have a word with you.' He stepped to one side with Richard, and Jane Pritchard smiled at Meryl.

'They never quite stop working, doctors, do they?' She smiled at Meryl. 'Have you been here in Millington long?'

'Most of my life,' Meryl told her. 'I grew up in this house.'

'Oh, of course—Taylor. You must be Dr Margaret's niece. I've heard about you.'

Meryl coloured. She supposed she had asked for that! 'Nothing too incriminating, I hope?' she asked crisply, and the other girl laughed.

'Ah, now that would be telling, wouldn't it?'

For the first time Meryl noticed a slight lilt to the girl's accent and realised with a small shock that she too was Welsh—of course, the name should already have given her a clue. Jane took a sip of her drink, her eyes following Gareth as he stood talking now to Maurice Dunster.

'Dr Owen-Thomas is *very* nice, isn't he?' she asked with an almost imperceptible sigh. Meryl looked at her sharply.

'Yes. I'm sure he'll be a great asset to the practice.' She cleared her throat. 'Do you and he come from the same place?'

Jane smiled. 'How clever of you to guess! Actually we have met before—once—though I don't think he re-members it. It was at a wedding in Wales about four years ago.'

'You'll be able to remind him of it this evening,' Meryl remarked. 'It'll make a nice talking point for you.'

*

It was after seven when Meryl arrived at Richard's flat that evening. She found him waiting. He had changed out of the smart grey suit into a pair of slacks and a tweed jacket, and she looked him up and down.

'Oh, I thought we were going out to dinner.'

'We are. I thought a country pub might be nice, though, after all that formality this afternoon.' He looked at her. 'You're looking a little tense. Is anything the matter?'

She shook her head. He came closer, putting his hands on her shoulders and looking down at her.

'Don't give me that. Something's up, isn't it? I haven't known you all these years without knowing when you're rattled. Is it the new practice nurse?'

She looked away from the probing blue eyes. 'I did find her personality a little grating. But I don't suppose I shall be coming into contact with her all that often. Anyway, what does my opinion count?'

He laughed at her gently. 'Now then, don't let's get paranoid about it, eh?'

'I'm not!' she looked at him. 'I mean it! I realise that I went over the top about Dr Owen-Thomas's appointment. Aunt Maggie gave me quite a talking to about it, and she was right. I'm a reformed character!'

He laughed and bent to kiss her briefly. 'Well, it doesn't suit you. If this is what it does to you I'd rather have the old Meryl back, even if it's only for this evening.' He slipped an arm round her shoulders, giving her a quick hug. 'Come on, let's go out and paint the town a delicate shade of puce if not bright red. Maybe you're just hungry. At least I know how to cure that!'

The country pub they chose was quiet, and when they had finished eating Richard looked at her enquiringly.

'Boring here, isn't it? I'm not as tired as I thought I was. It must be the sight of you in that dress. Green is definitely your colour.' He stood up and held out his hand. 'Come on—we're going.'

She looked at him in surprise. 'Going—where?'

'That new country club on the Northwich road,' he announced. 'I'm not letting you go to waste.'

'But it's late!'

'Not too late, though. We can have a drink and maybe a dance or two.' He grasped her hand and pulled her to her feet. 'Come on, I'm not taking no for an answer!'

Meryl hadn't been to the Pink Parrot before. It had only been open for a few months. Richard bought drinks and brought them to her at the table the waiter had found for them close to the tiny dance floor, and she stared at the bright pink liquid with its collection of tropical fruit and minuscule paper parasol.

'What on earth is this?' she gasped.

He grinned. 'Speciality of the house, Caribbean Sunset. Drink it up like a good girl. Maybe it'll lift that depression.'

She looked at him in dismay. 'Richard, once and for all, I am *not* depressed.'

He took a sip of his drink. 'No? You could have fooled me!'

She smiled at him apologetically. 'I'm sorry. I haven't been very good company, have I?'

He reached across the table to cover her hand with his. 'Is it living at the beach house? It must be lonely for you out there. It'll be even worse when the winter sets in. Look, I know the flat isn't very big, but you're welcome to share it if you want.' He gave her a rueful grin. 'No strings, of course. I need hardly say that to you after all the years we've known each other, need I?'

She gave his hand a squeeze. 'Richard, you are sweet. And I do appreciate the offer. It's nothing to do with the beach house, though. I quite like it there. I've even had several swims.'

'What, then?' He looked into her eyes. 'You know if there's anything I can do you have only to ask.'

She lifted her shoulders helplessly, searching for a satisfactory reply to his question. 'I honestly don't know. Maybe it was today—it was rather emotional for me, after all. I haven't really analysed my feelings, but I suspect that may have had something to do with it.'

Richard stood up and drew her to her feet. 'Come and dance.'

Reluctantly she allowed herself to be propelled on to the small dance floor where about a dozen couples were moving slowly round. For a few moments they danced in silence. Meryl began to relax with the music, then suddenly as Richard swung her round she stiffened. She found herself facing the entrance to the dining room, and a couple coming out caught her attention. The man was tall and striking, the girl, small and fair, looking adoringly up at him—Jane Pritchard, on the arm of Gareth Owen-Thomas. Her first instinct was to turn and run, but she could hardly do that. Instead she hid her face against Richard's shoulder. His arm around her waist tightened as he glanced down at her with pleasure. 'There, you've relaxed. I knew you would.'

She didn't speak, almost holding her breath. Perhaps they were on their way out and would go without noticing them. She was out of luck. Suddenly Richard exclaimed:

'Well, of all the luck! If it isn't the great man himself!'

Meryl looked round for some way of escape. 'Let's go,' she muttered, but Richard looked at her.

'We can't—they've seen us.'

He was right, Gareth was making his way towards them and waving. Richard greeted him warmly.

'Hello there! What a surprise, seeing you like this. Will you join us for a drink?'

Gareth smiled. 'That would be very nice.'

They all sat down at the table and Richard looked at Jane. 'What will you have?'

She looked at the untouched concoction in front of Meryl. 'What's that?'

Richard grinned. 'It's called a Caribbean Sunset. I can recommend it. Before she started drinking that poor old Meryl was quite down in the dumps. It's done wonders for her!'

Meryl blushed as Jane and Gareth turned to look at her. She forced a laugh.

'Take no notice of him—he's making it all up. I haven't even tried it yet! It's probably awful. If I were you I'd stick to whatever you usually have.'

Richard brought the drinks, then asked Jane to dance. Meryl sipped her Caribbean Sunset, trying not to look at Gareth, until he said:

'I'm sorry to hear you were depressed.'

'I wasn't really. That was just Richard's exaggeration.' She stared into her glass. 'I was right about this—it *is* awful.'

'I thought it went very well this afternoon, didn't you?'

'Yes. I'm rather relieved that it's all over, though. I don't like formal occasions much. It'll be nice to get down to some sort of normal routine.'

'You're right there.' He cleared his throat. 'We haven't seen much of each other since I moved in at the beach house.'

'No.' Meryl was unable to stop herself from colouring. 'By the way, I haven't mentioned it to anyone—I don't know if you—?'

'No, I haven't.' She bit her lip, noticing the amused expression in his eyes. Did he think her small-minded and old-fashioned?

'It's just that people might think—might get—'

'The wrong idea?' he supplied. 'Don't give it another thought. People in my part of the world can be narrow-minded too, you know. People in small towns usually are a bit that way, even in this day and age. I'm still looking for a place of my own, by the way.'

'Of course.'

'I wouldn't want you to think I was taking advantage of your good nature.'

'I'm sure you wouldn't do that.'

He smiled. 'Would you like to dance?'

To her surprise the request made her heart jump alarmingly and she tried to keep the startled expression out of her eyes.

'Thank you.'

They had just reached the edge of the dance floor when the music stopped. Gareth smiled and pressed her hand.

'Better luck next time.'

But Meryl was determined that there shouldn't be a next time; the thought of being in Gareth's arms again was too exciting for her peace of mind. As soon as Richard returned to the table with Jane Pritchard she looked at him.

'Richard, I really think we should be going. I have a heavy schedule tomorrow and I mustn't be too late.'

'Of course.' He got to his feet, looking apologetically at the others. 'Sorry about this. Maybe we can make up a foursome again some time. That is if we ever manage to be free again at the same time, eh?'

Meryl felt Gareth's eyes on her. 'Maybe we'll meet again soon, Meryl.'

She couldn't quite meet his gaze as she replied:

'Yes—perhaps.'

On the way home they drove in silence for a while, then Richard said:

'I think I know what's wrong with you, Meryl. And for once I hope I'm wrong. In fact I've never hoped for anything quite so much!'

CHAPTER FIVE

It was strange to be working at the Wellford Centre instead of at the hospital. Meryl looked round her new room with pride. It was all her own instead of having to share it with other therapists. At St Luke's the room she had occupied was also used by several others coming to take weekly or monthly clinics. This room was divided into two sections: a small, pleasant consulting room, with a large playroom for children adjoining. She left her desk to walk through the open glass door to the play area, looking at everything with pride, stroking the old rocking horse that Aunt Maggie had brought down from the attic and had restored. Meryl remembered riding him when she was a small child herself. He had belonged to her father and Aunt Maggie when they had been small; it felt good to have him here.

In one corner there was a sand pit and a table with materials for small patients to draw and paint; it had long been recognised that children's drawings could reveal a great deal about their inner worries and fantasies. Thinking of this reminded her of something, and she unzipped her briefcase and took out the drawings Mrs Venables had given her the day before when she was at St Winifred's. Sitting down at her desk, she unfolded them and smoothed them out. She had only just started to study them when the door opened and Gareth came in. Meryl looked up.

'Good morning.'

He smiled. 'Good morning. How does it feel to be here at last?'

'Wonderful!' She brought her eyes back to the drawings in front of her. Last night she had not heard Gareth come back to the beach house. For some time she had lain in bed, listening for the sound of his car—trying not to speculate about him and his companion. At last she must have fallen asleep, and this morning there had been no sign of him. She could only assume that he had not, in fact, come in at all, though she tried hard not to think about it. She was acutely aware of his nearness as he bent to look over her shoulder.

'What have we here—works of art from an adoring admirer?'

She shook her head. 'Mrs Venables gave them to me yesterday. She's the head of St Winifred's, the school for handicapped children. You may not have met her yet. These belong to a young patient—Peter Sopwith. He's starting at St Winifred's soon and she's rather concerned about him.'

Gareth leaned closer. 'Mmm—children's drawing can be very revealing. I did a psychology course soon after I qualified and for a time I worked in the psychiatric clinic at my hospital. I found it fascinating—in fact if I hadn't—'

He broke off as she turned to look up at him. 'Here, let me have a look.' He took the drawings from her and studied them carefully. 'He loves colour, doesn't he?' he observed. 'They're very dramatic—gory too. Do you notice that all the animals have been injured or broken in some way?' He held the drawings out and Meryl leaned over to look.

'Oh yes. What does that mean?'

He rubbed his chin. 'It could be one of several meanings. Do you have any notes for him?'

Meryl patted the pile of mail on her desk. 'Probably among this little lot.' She opened her appointment book and looked down the list. 'Yes, I'm seeing him tomorrow, so I expect they're here.'

He nodded. 'I'd hazard a guess that there's something wrong with relationships at home. Probably a splitting of the family in some way. Let me know if I'm right, eh?' He smiled. 'Did you have a good time last night?'

To her annoyance she found herself colouring. 'Yes, very nice, thank you—did you?'

'Oh yes, I did indeed. Going out for the evening rounded off the occasion nicely. What a coincidence that Sister Pritchard and I come from the same corner of Wales.'

'Yes, isn't it?'

'Good company makes all the difference, don't you feel?' he asked.

Meryl began to open her mail. 'Yes.'

Gareth perched comfortably on one corner of her desk. 'Have you and Jessel been going out together long?'

She looked up at him in surprise. 'No—at least, I don't consider us exactly 'going out together'. We've been friends since we were children.'

'I see.'

She looked at him, then pointedly at her watch. 'Is there anything special you wanted to see me about, Doctor? My clinic starts in fifteen minutes and I'd rather like to familiarise myself with the cases I'll be seeing before that.'

He stood up. 'Of course. No, nothing special. I just

wanted to welcome you. I've been round everyone now—you were last on the list. I'll leave you to it, then. Good luck.'

'Good luck to you too, Doctor!' Meryl pulled a face at the closed door as he went out. Welcome her indeed—to her own home! In spite of the fact that it was now a health centre is still felt like home to her. It always would, no matter how many brilliant Welsh doctors took it over! And what did it have to do with him how long she and Richard had been friendly?

She had just returned to her mail when the door opened again and her aunt slipped into the room.

'Good morning, dear. Well, how does it feel to be in your very own room?'

Meryl sighed. 'A bit like sitting in the middle of Piccadilly Circus, if you want to know! Ever since I got here I've had a constant stream of visitors asking me how it feels to have a room of my own!'

Margaret looked surprised. 'I'm sure that's a slight exaggeration. I take it you mean Gareth? I thought it was very sweet of him to go round everyone and wish them luck. I saw him coming out of here.'

'Yes, apparently I was last on the list,' Meryl told her wryly.

'How are you two getting along together at the beach house?' Margaret asked. Meryl shrugged.

'We aren't really. We hardly see one another, which is how I like it. It's bad enough having to work with the man.' She looked up at her aunt. 'Can't you ask around and see if you can find him a flat? I'm sure you know someone who could help.'

'I already have,' Margaret told her. 'But it isn't easy, as you know. Sister Pritchard is looking for a place too, though it isn't desperate. She seems quite comfortable where she is for the moment.'

'Mmm, that one would make herself at home wherever she was,' Meryl remarked.

Margaret looked sharply at her. 'I don't know what's come over you lately, Meryl. No one seems right for you. Perhaps you need a holiday. Richard is worried about you too. I was speaking to him only this morning, and he said you were quite out of sorts last night when he took you out to celebrate.'

Meryl suppressed the remark that rose to her lips and Margaret leaned across to pat her shoulder. 'I almost forgot what I came in for,' she said. 'Libby asked me to invite you for dinner. She thinks you need fattening up. How about next Friday?'

Meryl nodded resignedly. Everyone seemed determined to organise her life in one way or another! Well, why not let them think they could—why not humour them? It was easier than arguing.

'Fine,' she said. 'I'll look forward to it.'

The morning's clinic went well, both the small patients and their mothers appreciating the new relaxed atmosphere and facilities. When it was over Meryl put on her coat and drove round to St Luke's to see Mr Johnson. As she slipped into her white coat in Sister's office she learned that he had been out of bed and down to Jean Taggart in Physio for his exercises.

'He's really making good progress,' Sister told her, 'though of course his speech is slow.' She frowned. 'His wife isn't helping much there. She keeps on about the after-dinner speeches he used to make—in front of the poor man too! I think it upsets him.' She shook her head. 'Isn't it funny, the way some people think a person who can't speak can't *hear* either?'

Meryl smiled. 'Will Mrs Johnson be coming in this morning? I could have a word with her.'

Sister frowned. 'No. I told her not to come this morning—I thought she might spoil things for you. Do you want me to tell her you'd like to see her?'

Meryl opened her diary. 'No, perhaps it might be better if I were to call on her at home. Can you give me her address and telephone number? I'll try to fit it in.'

Without his wife Mr Johnson seemed bright and eager to do his exercises. Meryl went through the muscular and phonetic ones with him, then gave him tests to assess his powers of recognition. He seemed well able to recognise the objects she held up for him and she could see him attempting to form the words. By the time she left the ward she felt that progress was being made.

Meryl returned to the beach house that evening at about five-thirty. She knew Gareth was taking a late surgery, so she did not expect him back until about seven. She decided to use the time to wash her hair and do her laundry. It was awkward, sharing with a man. Another girl would understand her need to drip-dry her undies over the bath and to spend long periods of time in the bathroom, but with Gareth in the house she felt unable to indulge in these things. She had just finished drying her hair when the telephone rang. Running a comb through the auburn mass to prevent it from tangling, she went through to the living room to answer it. It was Richard.

'Hello—Meryl? Just thought I'd ring to make sure you were all right. I didn't get a chance to see you this morning—by the time I'd finished surgery you'd left for the hospital. I meant to look in and wish you luck.'

Meryl sighed. 'And to ask me how I liked the privacy of having my own room, no doubt,' she said ironically.

'What? How's that again?' Richard sounded puzzled and she said quickly:

'Never mind. Have you had a good day?'

'Great! To tell you the truth, I was a bit worried about you last night,' he went on. 'I didn't upset you, did I?'

Meryl sighed. 'No, you didn't. Why is everyone so concerned about my welfare suddenly?'

'Maybe it's because you don't seem yourself,' he told her. 'You haven't done for a couple of weeks. Ever since Owen-Thomas arrived here, in fact.' He cleared his throat. 'He—doesn't have anything to do with it, does he?'

'Now why should he? Just tell me that,' Meryl demanded. Suddenly the mention of Gareth reminded her of the time and she looked at her watch. He would be home at any minute now; Richard might even hear him. 'Hang on a minute,' she said. 'I'm going to switch this through to the bedroom—I was washing my hair, you see.' She ran upstairs and took the receiver off, shouting: 'Hang on a minute!' to Richard while she ran down again to replace the receiver. When at last she got back to him he sounded mystified.

'What on *earth* are you playing at?' he demanded.

'It's the extension,' she explained.

'You should have one of those new plug-in telephones,' he told her. 'Now, what I really rang for was to ask you out this evening.'

'But we went out last night!'

'I wasn't aware that dates with you were rationed,' he said dryly. 'Besides, last night was your idea. Tonight it's mine. A man does like to take the initiative sometimes, you know!'

'Sorry, Richard, I can't,' she apologised.

'Why?'

'I told you, I'm washing my hair. Anyway, late nights don't suit me. I'm tired. I owe it to the patients to get an early night tonight.'

'Sure?'

'Sure.'

'All right, then.' He hesitated. In the distance Meryl could hear a car coming slowly along the bumpy track. Richard spoke again: 'Would you like me to come out there and keep you company?'

'What? Oh, *no*!'

'All right, you needn't sound so horrified at the prospect!' His voice sounded wounded.

'I'm not. Look, I'm sorry, Richard, I have to go. I've got something on the stove and I think it's boiling over. I'll talk to you tomorrow.' As she put the receiver on its rest Meryl heard Gareth come in and slam the front door. She heaved a sigh. She was not a moment too soon. If only he would find himself somewhere else soon! Her nerves would be in shreds at this rate. The mistake she had made was in not being open to Richard about their sharing arrangement from the first; if she suddenly disclosed it now it would look odd. Suddenly she remembered the bathroom, festooned with her undies, and rushed to remove them.

She need hardly have bothered. After about half an hour Gareth went out again. She saw him leave the house from her window. He was looking very smart, dressed in expensive-looking grey slacks and a jacket that looked like handwoven tweed. Meryl pulled a wry face. No doubt he was meeting Sister Jane Pritchard again. That girl had wasted no time in assuring that Gareth would not forget her again in a hurry! She half wished she had agreed to go out with Richard now, then she pulled herself up sharply. What had she been expecting of this evening? Suddenly she hated Gareth Owen-Thomas *and* Sister Jane Pritchard. Before they came to Millington she had been a nice person with a generous, unsuspicious nature. They had brought out the worst in her!

After she had eaten she decided to have an early night. The evenings were already beginning to darken early, and soon the clocks would be put back for the winter. As she lay in bed, listening to the crash of the waves on the shore, she wondered what it would really be like here in the winter. Would Gareth still be here, or would he have found a place of his own by then? She found herself wondering how old he was—in his mid-thirties, she guessed—and why he had never married. Most of the doctors she knew seemed to marry at a fairly early age. She thought about Richard. Theirs was a platonic friendship—or so she had always thought. Lately, though, he seemed inordinately concerned with her welfare. She sincerely hoped he wasn't nursing any hopes of deepening their relationship; they knew each other far too well for that.

She must have fallen asleep over her book—only to be awakened some time later by a crash. With a start, she sat up in bed. The door was open, and she could see a man's form silhouetted against the pale square of moonlight coming from the landing window. She screamed. The light was snapped on and she came face to face with Gareth. He was dressed in a short towelling bathrobe and his hair was tousled from sleep.

'For heaven's sake, what's the matter with you? It's only me!' he said crossly.

Meryl stared at him, clutching the duvet to her throat. 'What are you doing? What do you want at this time of night?'

'For heaven's sake—what do you *think* I want? Didn't you hear the blasted telephone ringing? You must be stone deaf, woman!'

She blinked at him sleepily. 'Telephone? But it's downstairs.'

'You're right. Full marks!' he said sarcastically. 'The only snag is that some idiot had taken a call on this extension and forgotten to replace the receiver properly.'

Meryl clapped a hand over her mouth. 'Oh—I'm sorry. It was me.'

He ran a hand through his already ruffled hair. 'Well, fancy that! Surprise, surprise! And now that whoever it was has given up, what do you suggest—mental telepathy?'

She shook her head. 'There's no need to be so nasty about it. Don't you ever make mistakes?'

'I hope not where the welfare of a patient is at risk,' he said coldly.

She glared at him. 'Maybe I'll live long enough to attain your perfection, *Dr Owen-Thomas!*'

The ringing of the telephone at her side made her start and she reached out a hand to pick up the receiver, but Gareth was there before her, roughly dashing her hand out of the way.

'Hello—Dr Owen-Thomas here.'

Meryl listened, holding her breath. She hated to admit

it, but she was in the wrong. She hoped fervently that this was the same caller. Gareth asked:

'Did you ring a few moments ago?' He looked at her and nodded. 'Right, I'll be there as soon as I can.' He replaced the receiver. 'She thought perhaps she hadn't let it ring long enough and tried again. It's a small boy with an asthma attack. I'd better get going.'

When he had gone Meryl lay for a while listening to his rapid preparation. He left the house like a hurricane and a moment later she heard the sound of his car as it bumped along the track towards the road. She sighed. How could she have been so stupid? After insisting on having this room she should have been extra careful. Feeling wide awake, she tried to read for a while, but the words danced meaninglessly before her eyes. At last she got up and pulled on her dressing gown. She would go down and make herself a cup of tea. Perhaps she could leave some in a flask for Gareth—as a sort of olive branch.

She was just pouring the boiling water into the pot when she heard the slam of the front door and turned to see Gareth standing in the open kitchen doorway.

'Hello, what's this, insomnia?' he queried.

'I couldn't get back to sleep. Want a cup?'

'I'd love one—thanks.'

She arranged two cups on a tray and took down the biscuit tin, looking at him enquiringly. 'You weren't long. How was the patient?'

'He'll be fine. An injection and some oxygen, plus plenty of reassurance, was all that was needed.'

Meryl smiled with relief. 'I'm glad to hear it. Would you like a biscuit, or shall I make you a sandwich?'

His face broke into a disarming smile. 'That's very kind of you, but a biscuit will be fine.'

'I expect you had another big dinner,' she remarked.

'What makes you think that?'

She blushed. 'I—saw you going out earlier—dressed very smartly.'

'Thanks for the compliment! Didn't you know there was a practice meeting this evening?'

She shook her head. 'In that case you can't have had time to eat at all.'

'Sister Pritchard made me an omelette in the kitchen at Wellford House after surgery,' he told her casually.

Meryl sniffed. 'Oh.' She poured the tea and passed him a cup, and he looked at her speculatively.

'Is this your way of apologising, Meryl?'

She coloured. 'I suppose you might call it that. I didn't expect you back so soon, actually.' She glanced at him. 'I was going to leave you some in a flask.'

Gareth reached out to rest his hands on her shoulders. 'I'm sorry I shouted at you.'

'You were right—I was stupid and careless,' she admitted. 'I won't do it again.' She looked up at him, her face brightening. 'Tell you what, why don't you have my room? I know what I said, but it really doesn't matter where I sleep.'

He looked at her for a long moment, then slowly drew her towards him. She stared at him as though mesmerised, her heart beginning to beat fast. When his lips came down on hers they were warm and firm, and she responded eagerly. His arms slid round her, drawing her close. She wound her own arms around his neck, her fingers lacing into the thick hair at the nape of his neck. No kiss had ever affected her as this one did, and when at

last he released her she was trembling. He looked down
at her.

'Are you cold?'

She laughed shakily. 'No.'

He drew her close again, his lips once more seeking
hers, parting them to kiss more deeply, demanding her
response. It was as though her awareness was height-
ened, every sensation accentuated. She was acutely
aware of the roughness of his cheek, the pressure of his
hard body against hers, and her heart fluttered wildly as
she clung to him. The belt of her dressing gown fell loose
and she felt his hands slide inside to slip round her waist,
caressing her naked back.

'You're lovely, Meryl,' he whispered, his lips moving
sensuously against her ear. The breath caught in her
throat at the touch of her hands on her skin. Her head
fell back and she closed her eyes as she drew his head
down to hers again, her mouth soft and yielding beneath
his as he pressed her closer. Then suddenly he took her
face in his hands and stepped back. Kissing her briefly on
the forehead, he pulled the disordered dressing gown
tightly round her and tied the belt.

'Back to bed with you,' he whispered huskily, 'before
I forget myself. This won't do, will it?'

She stared up at him, swallowing hard. 'What is it?'
she whispered. 'What did I do?'

He shook his head, smiling wryly. 'You scared the
living daylight out of me, that's what you did. This is
your aunt's house, and she trusts me. I'm her partner.'

Meryl bit her lip hard. 'You're also an adult with a
mind of your own—as I am,' she said sharply. Gareth
shook his head.

'We're two normal healthy people who find ourselves

in a provocative situation. It's as well to be able to recognise that.'

Meryl frowned. 'How lucky you are to be able to view it with such clinical detachment. Good night!'

In her room she climbed into bed and pulled the duvet over her head. She had believed he meant the words he had whispered—each tender melting touch, but all he really saw her as was a temptation to be resisted—like a cream cake or a bag of toffees! Did he see her as a woman at all? Was he capable of normal masculine feelings? She bit her lip hard, hating herself for revealing a side of her nature she had scarcely known she possessed. 'Damn you, Gareth Owen-Thomas,' she muttered through clenched teeth. 'Damn you!'

CHAPTER SIX

MERYL heard the rain next morning the moment she opened her eyes. She peered at the clock and pulled the duvet over her head for another five minutes. Then as she lay listening to the rain dripping from the roof the memory of the previous evening slowly seeped back into her consciousness. Even as she remembered Gareth's kiss her heart lurched. She checked herself quickly. If she wasn't very careful she would find herself falling in love, and that would mean disaster. Obviously he had no intention of marrying anyone, but he quite clearly appreciated feminine company—she refused to put it more strongly, even to herself. Well, she would show him that two could play at that game. He didn't have the monopoly on playing the field!

As she made herself a hasty breakfast Gareth did not put in an appearance. The house was silent. Maybe he had had another call and gone out while she was still asleep. Whatever it was, she was grateful for it. To have faced him over breakfast would have been humiliating and embarrassing.

She had a later clinic that morning, and on her way to the Centre she called on Mrs Johnson. As she pulled up outside the neat detached house she paused to think of how she would tackle the situation. She didn't want to upset her patient's wife, that might only make things more difficult for him, but it was intolerable that he should be made to feel guilty for his slow progress. As she rang the front doorbell she still hadn't worked out what she would say, so she decided to play it by ear. There was a very long pause before the door was answered and Meryl began to think Mrs Johnson must have risen early and gone out, but at last the door opened a fraction and a startled face peered out. Mrs Johnson was still in her dressing gown.

'Oh—Miss Taylor, it's you!'

Meryl smiled. 'I'm sorry to call on you so early, Mrs Johnson, but I wanted to have a word with you about your husband!'

'Oh! He isn't worse—you haven't come with bad news?'

Meryl bit her lip. How could she have been so tactless? 'No, no, nothing like that. He's fine. May I come in, please?'

The woman held the door open. 'Of course, how rude of me, keeping you standing on the doorstep.' She led the way to a pretty sitting room. 'Please, sit down. Maybe you'd like a coffee.' She looked at Meryl shyly. 'You'll think me terrible—still not dressed at this time of the morning! To tell you the truth, I didn't sleep very well and I was having a bit of a lie-in.'

Meryl laid a hand on her arm. 'Look, would you like me to leave it until another day?'

'No—please. It's nice to have someone to talk to. Early in the morning and last thing at night—they're the worst times, you know.'

'I'm sure Mr Johnson will soon be home with you now.' Meryl took a deep breath. 'Actually, that's partly why I've come to see you.' She sat down, and Mrs Johnson sank on to the settee opposite.

'Do you have some news?' she asked eagerly.

'No, just advice really. I hope you won't think I'm intruding on your privacy, Mrs Johnson, but when your husband does come home life could be tricky for a little while—until you both readjust.'

The older woman looked puzzled. 'Of course—I realise that. But he will improve, won't he? And it's my job to help him as much as I can.'

Meryl nodded. 'That's right, but the *way* you help is all-important. The main thing to remember is that the life you had before is a closed chapter. The future can be just as good—but different.'

Mrs Johnson sighed. 'What you're trying to say is that he'll never be the same again, aren't you?'

'In a way,' Meryl agreed. 'That's something we all face at some time or other. Every traumatic experience changes us, and a stroke is perhaps the biggest trauma anyone ever has to face. It *is* possible that he'll make a complete recovery, many people do, but don't try to rush him, and don't make him feel a failure if he doesn't get on as quickly as you want him to.'

Mrs Johnson blushed. 'That Sister at the hospital has been talking to you, hasn't she? Did she ask you to come?'

Meryl shook her head. 'We have to work together on each case, and she did mention that you were worried about the rate of his progress. That's very natural. You had a happy life, and you're anxious to have him home again and back to normal.'

'So you're saying that I should ease up on helping him?'

'Just go along with each new step he takes,' Meryl advised. 'Encourage but don't push.' She smiled. 'I know it isn't easy, but I promise you, it'll pay off.'

The morning clinic was for adults, and for the first time Paul Dixon came, brought by his wife. He was to join a group this morning, but when he arrived he seemed anxious and ill at ease.

'Paul has just been up for his physiotherapy,' Julie Dixon told Meryl. 'I must say it's easier, having everything in one building.'

'How is he?' asked Meryl. Julie shook her head.

'Still short-tempered. It's hard sometimes to keep calm.' She gave Meryl an apologetic smile. 'To be honest, there are times when I could hit him with something!'

'Well, why don't you?' The other girl looked shocked and Meryl added: 'You mustn't let him get away with everything, you know. He's had a tough time, but he's making good progress. I understand he can take a few steps unaided now?'

Julie sighed. 'But it's all so slow—too slow for Paul. And knowing that he'll never do the things he did before—sport and so on—'

'Tell him how lucky he is,' Meryl urged. 'He *is*, you know. Plenty of people who have been through accidents like he had never walk again. When he gets stroppy give him a good talking to. Let him know you get tired and fed up too.' She smiled. 'Look, while he's here why don't you go off and do some shopping—have a coffee or get your hair done? It'll do you good.'

'But what if he's ready and I'm not here?'

'It won't be the end of the world! He can sit in the waiting room and look at a magazine. It won't hurt him,' Meryl told her. 'As a matter of fact there's someone I'd like him to meet. Go on, think of yourself for an hour. It'll do you good.'

The group was a small one. Seated in a circle round
Meryl, they repeated their exercises—for the lips, jaw
and tongue, followed by the articulatory ones—blowing
and repeating the sounds p,b,m,w, and f. At first Paul
seemed acutely embarrassed. He was used to the exercises, but doing them in company seemed to make him
feel uncomfortable. Meryl noticed that he seemed unable to perform some things which so far he had managed well, but she made no comment. In her opinion this
young man was growing thoroughly spoiled. At the end
of the session she decided to introduce him to another
young man, first taking him aside to tell him Graham's
story.

'I'd like you to meet Graham Jenkins,' she said
quietly. 'He's about your age and he was in an accident
very like yours, except that—tragically—his fiancée was
with him and she was killed. He lives with his elderly
father who doesn't have very good health himself, so
he's had to get well as quickly as possible. If you get
along well maybe you could ask him round to your house
for tea one day. I think he'd appreciate that.'

Paul looked round as though trying to find an excuse
to escape. He made it clear to Meryl that his wife would
be waiting for him. She shook her head.

'Julie went to do some shopping, and I told her to take
her time. So you've plenty of time to get acquainted with
Graham. He's not lucky enough to have his own car, like
you—he has to wait for his transport to collect him, and
sometimes it's quite a long wait. You can sit in the
waiting room. I'll give you some paper and pencils.
Luckily you're both able to write.'

By the time Julie Dixon returned to pick up her
husband she found him smilingly conversing with the

young man Meryl had told her about. Her hair was newly shampooed and blow-dried and she looked prettier and more relaxed than Meryl had seen her since they first met. When Paul looked up and saw her it was clear that he appreciated the change too. As she watched them leave Meryl heaved a sigh. Sometimes she wondered if she interfered too much. She hated to see her patients unhappy, though, and often a stranger saw more than a close relative. But she sometimes wondered why she wasn't told to 'mind her own business' more!

During the afternoon clinic Meryl met the little boy Mrs Venables had told her about and whose drawings she had been studying. He was a well developed, good-looking child, and Meryl sent him off to the playroom while she talked with his mother. The first thing she learned was that the parents had separated and were in the process of a divorce.

'I honestly don't think that's the cause of Peter's trouble, though,' Mrs Sopwith told Meryl. She looked down at the hands that were clenched in her lap. 'John wasn't a good father. He never took any interest in Peter. I'm sure we're both better off without him.'

'Has Peter mentioned your husband at all since he left?' Meryl asked. The woman shook her head.

'Not once—that's what makes me think he isn't affected by it. But his speech is definitely getting worse. Sometimes even I can't understand what he's trying to say.'

'And his speech had developed quite normally up till recently?'

'Perfectly. In fact he was extremely forward as a baby.'

Meryl let Peter play during the afternoon clinic; drawing seemed to be his favourite occupation, but he liked modelling with the sand and plasticine too. She noticed that he paid little attention to the other children, though when she talked to him he was friendly enough. His mother was right, his speech was badly impaired, but she managed to make out his explanation of the pictures he produced. Again there were wounded animals, but today there was a tall man and a short one. There was also a sea full of man-eating sharks. Peter told her that the tall man was called Frank and that he could swim, but the little man couldn't. However, it was a good job the little man wasn't going in the water, because the sharks would get Frank. When his mother came to collect him, Peter told her that he had enjoyed his afternoon and asked if he could come again. Just before they left Meryl asked Mrs Sopwith:

'Do you know anyone called Frank?'

Mrs Sopwith coloured. 'Yes, as a matter of fact. That's the name of my boy-friend. He works on the rig.'

'Does Peter get along well with him?'

Mrs Sopwith nodded. 'Oh yes—very well.'

'I see. That's good. It's just that he mentioned someone called Frank when he was playing.'

When they had gone Meryl slipped Peter's drawings into her briefcase. She would study them later, at home. Maybe she would even ask Gareth's opinion.

But she didn't get the chance. She didn't see Gareth to speak to for several days. Perhaps he was avoiding her. Once or twice on her way out of Wellford House she heard his voice as he talked with Jane Pritchard in the nurse's room. Twice she heard them laughing together and was shocked at her reaction. As far as she could remember she had never suffered the emotion of jealousy in her life, but she was suffering it now, and she resented it deeply.

On Friday she found herself looking forward with pleasant anticipation to Libby's home-cooked dinner. All week she had existed on snack meals, never seeming to have the time or the interest to cook properly.

She arrived at Woodbine Cottage before her aunt and joined Libby in the kitchen, donning an apron and helping her as she had done in the old days when they had all lived together. The housekeeper looked her up and down. 'You're not dieting or anything stupid like that, are you?'

Meryl shook her head. 'I don't seem to need to.'

Libby sniffed. 'I'm not surprised! I expect you live on that awful junk food, full of nasty chemicals. Enough to waste anyone away, they are. Nothing to beat plenty of fresh fruit and vegetables, I say.'

'That's all right if you have time to prepare them,' Meryl protested.

Libby waved a wooden spoon at her. 'If you got up half an hour earlier you could make yourself a casserole and cook it in one of those slow cookers. It'd be ready for you when you came home. Or you could buy yourself a pressure cooker.'

Meryl pulled a face. 'I'm always afraid they'll blow up.' She lifted a saucepan lid. 'What have you made?'

Libby smiled. 'Your favourite—roast beef, with roast potatoes and sprouts.'

'Yorkshire pudding?' asked Meryl hopefully, and the housekeeper nodded.

'What else? I've made one of my lemon meringue

pies to follow. If that doesn't put a few pounds on you, I don't know what will!' She peered into the oven, then looked at Meryl speculatively. 'What about Dr Owen-Thomas—don't you cook for him?'

Meryl laughed. 'You have to be joking! Why should I cook for him?'

Libby shrugged. 'I thought you might enjoy it. You used to be a very good cook when we were all at Wellford House. You should be—*I* taught you, didn't I? I just thought it might be nice for you both.'

Meryl helped herself to an apple from the bowl on the dresser and bit into it. 'He gets his own meals, like me. We both work, why shouldn't he? Anyway, we keep different hours.'

Libby didn't look at her as she asked: 'How do you get along with him now?'

'I hardly see him,' Meryl replied noncommittally. 'I suppose he's all right in his way.'

She stopped munching her apple to look closely at the housekeeper. Her face had gone pink and she couldn't meet Meryl's eyes. Why? What was going on? But before she had time to ask her the front door slammed and she heard her aunt call out:

'Libby! Isn't Meryl here yet?'

'I'm here—helping with the dinner.' Meryl popped her head round the kitchen door in time to see her aunt taking off her coat in the hall. Margaret held out her hand.

'Come into the sitting room and have a sherry. Libby won't mind. When we've had it we'll lay the table together.'

As they sipped their sherry Margaret asked: 'Are you comfortable at the beach house?'

Meryl nodded. 'I like it there, though I'd prefer to have it to myself.'

Margaret shook her head. 'It's better to have company. It's a very lonely spot out there, especially in winter.'

'I don't mind solitude—and I still don't think it's a good idea, Gareth sharing with me. People are going to get to know some way or other very soon and then what will they think?'

'You should have been open about it from the start,' her aunt said. She looked shrewdly at her niece. 'You—get on well with him now, don't you?'

'I suppose so.'

'Better than you did in the beginning, I mean?'

Meryl frowned. 'I haven't come here to discuss Dr Owen-Thomas—I get enough of him all week. Let's relax, shall we?'

Libby's dinner lived up to Meryl's expectation of it. When she had finished she sat back contentedly.

'I don't think I could eat another crumb for a week!'

Libby sniffed disapprovingly as she poured coffee. 'I don't suppose you will either, if I know anything about your eating habits!' She looked at Margaret. 'I've been telling her, she should cook for Dr Gareth. That way they'd both eat properly. Nothing like having a man to feed, I say.'

Margaret smiled. 'I agree with you, Libby, though I dare say Meryl's generation would strongly disapprove.'

'All this silly Women's Lib nonsense!' Libby muttered to herself as she went out of the room. 'What were women put on this earth for, I'd like to know—if it wasn't to please men?'

As the door closed behind her Margaret and Meryl looked at each other, then burst out laughing.

'The perfect answer to a male chauvinist pig's prayer!' Margaret chuckled.

A moment later Libby was back, closing the door behind her conspiratorially.

'It's that Sister Pritchard at the door,' she announced. 'She wants to see you. Are you at home?'

'Of course. Ask her if she'd like to join us for coffee, and bring another cup, would you, Libby?'

The housekeeper looked doubtful, but went off, opening the door again a moment later to admit Jane.

'I'm awfully sorry to interrupt your meal,' she said. 'I won't stay long. I wouldn't have come, only it's rather an emergency.'

Margaret smiled. 'It's quite all right, it's only the two of us. Sit down and tell me what's worrying you.'

Jane sighed as she took a seat at the table. 'It's my digs. My landlady's given me notice, and she wants me to leave as soon as possible. Her son is coming home, you see. He's got a job nearer home and so of course she wants to make room for him. I wondered if you knew of anywhere?'

Margaret frowned. 'Oh dear, that is bad news. Don't worry, though. If the worst comes to the worst I can always put you up here temporarily.'

'Thanks. I'll ask around too, of course. I wouldn't like to put you and your housekeeper to any trouble.'

Libby came in with another cup and Margaret poured Jane a coffee. 'How are you liking it here in Millington —apart from the accommodation problem?' she asked.

Jane smiled. 'I like it very much. It's a nice bonus

having someone from my own part of the world to work with too.'

'You get along well with Dr Owen-Thomas, then?' Margaret asked, and Jane smiled.

'Oh yes. Of course I know a lot about him—maybe more than he thinks. You can't live in a small place like Llanmore Vale without knowing everyone's business.' She looked at Meryl and Margaret as though waiting for them to ask her to go on. When they didn't she continued anyway: 'For instance, did you know that he was almost married a few years back?'

Margaret shook her head. 'No, I didn't know that.'

'Oh yes. A medical student, she was. They studied together. But she had ambitions, and she ditched Gareth for the son of a Harley Street specialist. Of course, I think he's always been a little afraid of marriage—his parents, you know.'

Meryl looked at her aunt and saw that she had gone rather pink.

'What about his parents?' she asked.

Jane looked from one to the other. 'You mean you don't know about *that* either? He's very close, Gareth, isn't he?' She leaned across the table confidentially. 'Well, they split up, you know—years ago, when Gareth was still at school. His father was an engineer. He's retired now—lives in a little bungalow by the sea, in Tenby—lovely, they say it is.' She drank the last of her coffee and stood up. 'Well, I won't outstay my welcome. No doubt you two have family things to discuss.' She looked at her watch. 'I have a date anyway, so I'd better go and change. Thanks for your help, Dr Margaret.'

When she had gone Margaret looked at Meryl, eyebrows raised.

'I wonder if she gets to know as much about everyone she comes into contact with?'

Meryl shook her head. 'I think Gareth is a subject close to her heart. I wouldn't mind betting he's the date she spoke of.'

Margaret looked surprised. 'Really? Oh dear! I don't think those two are at all suited to one another.'

Meryl reached for the coffee pot and poured herself another cup, glancing sideways at her aunt. 'Did you know about Gareth's father and mother parting?' she asked.

'No.' Margaret got quickly to her feet and began to stack the dishes. 'Shall we give Libby a hand with these? She isn't getting any younger, you know.'

Meryl rose to help. Was it her imagination, she wondered, that Aunt Maggie looked flustered and embarrassed?

When Meryl arrived back at the beach house that night it was still raining. She put the car away in the garage and ran the twenty yards to the house. Inside, she slammed the front door and stood in the hall regaining her breath. Gareth's car had been in the garage and she was just wondering whether he had gone to bed when the kitchen door opened and he looked out, a mug of steaming coffee in his hand.

'Hello there. Want a coffee?—I've just made some. You're wet.'

Meryl smiled wryly, looking at herself in the hall mirror. 'Very observant of you!' Her hair hung in wet, curling tendrils about her face and droplets of rain still trickled down her nose.

Gareth handed her a handkerchief. 'Here, this any

use? It is a clean one, I promise.'

She took it gratefully and dabbed at the raindrops, following him into the kitchen. It smelled of an appetising meal, recently cooked. So he had been in this evening?

'I've been to dinner at Aunt Maggie's,' she told him. 'If there's one thing I miss, it's Libby's cooking.'

He glanced at her. 'Independence starting to pall a bit?'

'No, of course not!' she told him indignantly.

'You could always learn to cook yourself. I'm told there are some excellent evening courses.'

'I *can* cook, thank you very much. Libby taught me. It's simply a matter of time.'

Gareth placed a mug of coffee in front of her on the table. 'Or organisation. There are ways and means of eating well, you know. How do you think working wives manage?'

'I haven't the least idea. And as I have no intention of getting married I don't suppose I'll ever know,' she told him loftily.

He grinned. 'Spoken like a true feminist! Of course, it's all right for women nowadays, but I have a sneaking idea that people still expect a man to be married—especially a doctor.'

Meryl took a sip of her coffee. 'I'm sure you're right. In fact, now that you mention it, I was rather surprised at the committee appointing an unmarried doctor as senior here.'

'Perhaps you'd like to help me find a wife?'

She coloured. Was he teasing her? But his face was serious. 'Surely that's something that only you could do. Anyway, I don't know any girls of that kind.'

'What kind? Do prospective wives belong in a special category?'

Meryl swallowed hard. He *was* teasing her. She stood up and went to rinse her coffee mug at the sink. 'I really wouldn't know. I haven't the faintest idea what a man like you would expect in a wife, and even if I did—' She turned and stopped in mid-sentence as she found him facing her. Her heart gave a lurch and just for a split second she wanted to turn and run, then she remembered something and crossed the kitchen to pick up her handbag.

'I almost forgot,' she said brightly, 'I brought Peter Sopwith's drawings to show you. You might be able to help me interpret them. Look.' She spread the drawings out on the table and Gareth came to look.

'Mmm—interesting. What did you make of him?'

'He's a pleasant enough child, though his speech is very badly impaired. I think he's been badly teased by his schoolmates. At least he won't have to contend with that at St Winifred's.' She looked at him. 'You were right about the parents, by the way, they have split up. The mother has a new boy-friend too. His name is Frank.' She pointed to the large man in the drawing. 'This is supposed to be him, I think.'

'I see. I take it the little fellow here is Peter himself.'

'He didn't actually say so, but I imagine you're right. This water is the sea and those animals with the teeth are sharks. Peter told me that Frank can swim and the 'little man' can't, but that when Frank goes into the water the sharks will get him.'

Gareth turned to look at her. 'It's fairly obvious, isn't it? Peter is jealous of Frank because he's competition for his mother's attention. Peter probably feels inadequate, but doesn't understand why. Does he miss his father?'

Meryl shook her head. 'His mother says not. Apparently he never mentions him.'

'Mmm—that doesn't necessarily mean anything. It could be too hurtful for him to talk about. Who is his doctor?'

Meryl glanced at her notes and smiled. 'You are, as a matter of fact.'

'You mean he's been transferred to my list? I'd like to see him. Will you suggest—tactfully, mind—that she brings him for a visit some time in the near future? I'm sure we can help him, poor little chap.'

'I'll do that.' Meryl gathered her notes and the drawings together and put them away. 'I suppose I'd better go to bed. It's getting late.'

Gareth touched her arm. 'Meryl, I'm sorry about the other night.'

She shrugged, colouring slightly. 'So am I.'

He frowned. 'Would you like me to leave?'

'No!' She had said it before she had time to think —almost an automatic reaction. She blushed furiously.

Tentatively he put his hands on her shoulders. 'I have a lot of respect and admiration for you, Meryl.'

She couldn't keep the bitterness out of her voice. 'That's nice!'

She felt his fingers tighten on her shoulders and when she looked up she caught a flash of impatience in his eyes.

'Have I said the wrong thing *again*?' he demanded. 'What is it you want? To have your cake and eat it, I suppose!'

She pulled away from him. 'I don't know what you're talking about. As far as I know we're simply tenants of this house, sharing and trying to keep out of each other's hair as much as possible.'

'And not succeeding!' He grasped her shoulders again and jerked her to him. 'Keeping out of each other's hair, as you put it, is the last thing we're doing—I hope you're going to allow yourself to be feminine enough to admit that, at least! We're attracted to each other, Meryl. What are we going to do about it? That's what I want to know.'

Her heart was beating fast. 'How should I know? What do you usually do in similar situations? There must have been many!'

His brow darkened. 'And just what's *that* supposed to mean?'

She stared up at him. 'You can't have got to your age without having plenty of girl-friends.'

For a moment Gareth looked taken aback. 'A few—yes.'

'Well then, what do you usually expect of them?'

He shrugged. 'Companionship—friendship—' He shook his head. 'Damn it, Meryl, are you always this direct?'

'You asked me a straight question. I assumed you wanted a straight answer! So it's companionship and friendship you're after—nothing more than that.'

He grinned. 'Put like that it does sound rather dull, doesn't it?'

In spite of herself she found her lips twitching and the next moment the tension dissolved into laughter. Gareth's hands moved from her shoulders to frame her face.

'You look completely different when you laugh,' he told her softly, looking down into her eyes. 'I'd like to see it happen more often. You take yourself far too seriously, you know.'

Meryl swallowed. Odd things were happening to her breathing. 'Do I? What do you suggest I do about it?'

He didn't reply, but drew her close. His lips found hers, softly at first, then harder, more demandingly, till she could scarcely breathe. The intensity of her response made her head reel, and when his lips left hers and he held her close she heard herself murmuring his name, her lips against his neck. He bent to bury his face in her hair, his lips brushing her ear, dropping a line of fleeting kisses along the line of her jaw and downwards to press warmly against the throbbing pulse at the base of her throat. She caught her breath, letting her head fall back, lips parted, eyes closed. He kissed her again, deeply and intimately and she clung to him, her heart beating fast.

'You're so lovely, Meryl, so warm and beautiful,' he muttered against her hair. 'But I can't embark on a relationship with you here, in this house, much as I want to. It would seem like a betrayal of trust. You do understand that, don't you?'

She stared up at him, shattered by the sense of anti-climax. 'No—frankly, I don't. I can't see what a house has to do with the way two people feel or behave. Either you want me or you don't.'

'I'll be getting a place of my own quite soon,' he told her. 'On my own ground everything will seem right —above board.'

She pulled away from him angrily. 'Really? Goodness knows where *I* shall be by then. I may not even be in Millington—I've been thinking very seriously about applying for another job lately.'

Gareth grasped her shoulders and pulled her to him

roughly. 'Don't be stupid and arrogant! Listen, I want to look at some of the houses on the list the estate agent sent me this evening—there's one—'

She pulled away from him. 'I don't want to hear. It seems to me that if you find me as *resistible* as that you might as well not bother.' She stopped on her way out of the kitchen. 'Ask Jane Pritchard if she'd like to share your new house. I heard this evening that she's desperate for somewhere to live. It's quite clear she's only waiting to fall into your arms too. I hope you'll both be very happy! Good night!'

In her room she slammed the door and locked it as loudly as she could, then she undressed quickly and climbed miserably into bed. Gareth Owen-Thomas was a cold fish! How could he control his emotions so calmly? The way he spoke, he might have been planning a summer holiday or a fishing trip instead of a love affair. Why couldn't she have trusted her first instinct about him? And why did she feel so wounded? Tomorrow she would ring Richard and ask him to take her out for the day. She could relax and have fun with him. Yes, that was what she'd do. Who needed Gareth Owen-Thomas anyway? Let him find himself a new house. *She* would never set foot in it—not if he begged her on his knees!

When she awoke the sun was shining in through her window. She got up and threw it open, leaning out as far as she could. It was a beautiful blue and golden autumn day—perhaps the last warm sun they would see for a while. She looked at her watch; it was eight o'clock. She made up her mind on impulse. She would go for a swim. Taking her bikini from the drawer, she slipped into it, then, taking a towel, she ran down and let herself out of the house. There wasn't a soul about except her. It was just as she liked it—the whole beach to herself. The water was quite cold and for the first moment it took her breath away, but after that it felt clean and refreshing as she cut smoothly through it.

She had been swimming for perhaps ten minutes when she heard a voice hailing her, and looking round, she saw another swimmer coming towards her. He waved.

'Hi, Meryl! It was such a lovely morning I thought I'd come and dig you out. Great minds think alike, eh? You beat me to it!'

She laughed. 'Richard! I was going to ring you later.'

He caught up to her and splashed playfully. 'Ring me, eh? What about?'

'To see if you were doing anything today. You're not on call, are you?'

He shook his head. 'No.' He gave a shudder. 'God! This water isn't as warm as it looked. Any breakfast going at the house?'

She bit her lip. 'Well—'

'Come on—race you back!' And he was gone before she could think of an excuse.

She caught him up in the shallows. 'Look, Richard, suppose we go back to your flat for breakfast? I—forgot to go shopping yesterday and there isn't much in.'

He shook his wet hair. 'That's all right, coffee and toast will do me.'

'Well, I—'

Suddenly he laughed and gave her a push. She lost her balance and fell into the water again and Richard grasped her shoulders playfully.

'Now—breakfast or a ducking. Which is it to be?'

'What the *hell* do you think you're doing?'

They both turned at the loud angry voice, and Meryl's heart sank. Running across the sand was Gareth. He looked angry and threatening, his unshaven face dark with stubble and his dressing gown open to the waist. Richard stared at him.

'I might well ask you the same question!' he retorted.

CHAPTER SEVEN

MERYL stood there speechlessly as the two men stared at each other, then Gareth laughed.

'Jessel! I didn't recognise you. When I looked out of the window all I saw was someone in the water with Meryl, as I thought, attacking her.'

Richard waded out of the water and picked up his towel. 'I see. It was a case of "gallant doctor to the rescue," was it?'

His smile was relaxed, but Meryl knew him well enough to detect the acid note in his voice. She saw too the accusing look in his eyes as he turned to her where she still stood, up to her waist in the water.

'You'd better go in and have a hot shower, Meryl. You'll be catching your death of cold, as Libby would say.'

Gareth looked at her. 'I agree, you're blue with cold.' He bent and picked up her towel, holding it out to her, but she ran out of the water, ignoring it, brushing furiously past his outstretched arm.

When she emerged from the bathroom, dressed in jeans and a warm sweater, she found Gareth in the kitchen. An appetising aroma of bacon met her nostrils, and he turned to her with a smile.

'There's a plate of bacon and eggs in the oven for you. You should eat something after your swim.'

She stood staring at him across the table. 'Why

on earth did you have to do a thing like that?' she demanded.

He shook his head. 'Like what? Oh, you mean out there on the beach? I told you, I thought some fool was attacking you. I got quite a shock. I looked out of the window and there you were in the water, being held under by this hulking brute. What was I supposed to do—leave you to drown?'

'I don't believe you,' she said. 'It isn't that far away. Surely you could see it was Richard?'

'He had his back to me. Anyhow, it's all right, he didn't seem offended. Anyone might have made the same mistake.'

'Where is he, by the way?' she asked.

'Gone home to breakfast, I should think. I did invite him to have it with us, but he—'

'You *what*?' Meryl was so angry she stamped her foot, and for the first time Gareth seemed to see her point.

'Ah!—Didn't he know I was sharing the house with you? Is *that* why you're so annoyed?'

'Of *course* it is. How can you be so stupid? Really —for a doctor—'

'But I thought you and he were "just good friends", as the saying goes.'

'We are—and I'd have liked us to stay that way. We *were* going out together for the day today—but now—'

Gareth reached across the table to take her hand, drawing her round to the chair he had pulled out for her. 'Look, sit down and eat the breakfast I've cooked for you. Afterwards you can drive round to Richard's flat and explain. I'll come with you if you like.'

Reluctantly she sat down. 'No, thanks. You've done enough damage for one day.'

'Let me take you out to lunch afterwards,' he said suddenly. 'I'm taking the emergency surgery this morning, but I'm free for the rest of the day. What do you say?'

Meryl looked up at him. He had shaved and dressed since she saw him on the beach, and he wore crisp grey slacks and a white shirt. She noticed the small cleft in his chin and the way his thick, dark hair curled into the nape of his neck, and for some strange reason these things made her heart lurch. Suddenly she found herself blushing—remembering with alarming clarity the way his lips had felt on hers, the tingling touch of his fingers on her skin. She swallowed hard, wishing the memory wasn't so profoundly disturbing.

'Well, does it take *that* much thinking about?' His eyes twinkled as they looked down into hers. 'I really am sorry about Richard, Meryl,' he told her earnestly. 'But if he thinks about it he'll realise how innocent the whole thing is. If it were some hole-and-corner affair I would hardly have acted as I did, now would I?'

'No. Anyway, Richard isn't my keeper. I shall tell him so too!'

He grinned. 'That sounds more like the Meryl Taylor we all know and love! Have your breakfast, then drive round to Richard's. I'll meet you in the lounge of the Bunch of Grapes at one-thirty. All right?'

She found herself agreeing—then hungrily attacking the piled-up plate he put before her. He left the house while she was still eating and she sat for a while, pondering over what had happened. She had meekly agreed to have lunch with him—and after the awful gaffe he had made earlier on the beach, causing her God only knew what embarrassment! She must be going soft in the head! Either that or—But the alternative was too terrifying to contemplate.

When he answered the door to her ring Richard looked surprised. 'Oh, it's you?'

Meryl walked inside and closed the door behind her. 'Well, aren't you going to offer me a cup of coffee?'

He shrugged. 'If you like. I suppose you've come to explain?'

She stared at him. 'Explain? Why should I want to do that? If you mean about Gareth's being at the beach house Aunt Maggie would be a better person to explain it to you—if that's necessary.'

'Your aunt?'

'Yes. It was her idea. Gareth was let down over accommodation and she gave him a key to the house. Without asking me first, I might add.'

Richard frowned. 'That doesn't sound like her.'

Meryl laughed shortly. 'Aunt Maggie's been doing quite a lot of things lately that aren't "like her", as you put it. The whole thing has been rather embarrassing. I suppose I should have been open about it from the first, but I don't see why I should go round explaining to people anyway—do you?'

Richard opened his mouth to say something, then appeared to change his mind. 'I'll make that coffee,' he said, turning in the direction of the kitchen. As he spooned coffee into the filter machine he asked: 'You said something about ringing me. What was it you wanted to ask?'

Meryl caught her breath. She had completely forgotten that she had intended to ask Richard to take her out for the day.

'Oh, it was nothing really,' she said. 'Just that we haven't seen much of each other lately. I thought it might be nice to have a chat.'

He smiled at her. 'Why don't we go out—spend the day together? We could take a picnic like we used to do. It would be fun.'

She looked at him regretfully. 'Oh, Richard, I'd love that—but I can't.'

He looked crestfallen. 'Got a date?' She nodded. He looked at her for a moment, lips pursed. 'It's him, isn't it—Owen-Thomas? I could see the way the wind was blowing right from the first. Are you in love with him?'

Meryl forced a laugh. 'Don't be such an idiot! I don't have to be madly in love with every man I go out with, do I?'

Richard lifted his shoulders. 'You've certainly never been in love with *me*.'

She winced inwardly. 'We've never had that kind of relationship, Richard. You know we haven't,' she said uncomfortably.

'Relationships can change,' he told her. 'People— *feelings* can change. We're not kids any more. For some time now I'd been hoping—' The last of the water filtered through with a loud slurp and he turned to the fridge for milk. 'I'd better shut up before I make a prize wally of myself.'

Meryl bit her lip. 'I wish you hadn't said all that, Richard,' she said slowly. 'You're the best friend I've ever had. I wanted it to stay that way for always.'

He shrugged, giving her a wry smile. 'Sorry to let you down. Of course I don't want our friendship spoiled. It *has* been known for people to be friends as well as lovers, you know.'

She looked at him wistfully. 'If it's any consolation, I'd rather be in love with you than anyone else I know.'

He pulled a face. 'But you're not—so it isn't.'

As Meryl drove into town later she felt sad. It was as though she had entered a new phase of her life. She and Richard had always been such good friends; now their relationship would never be quite the same. She had meant it when she said she would rather be in love with him than anyone else. Marriage to Richard would be such a comfortable, relaxed state. She sighed. What was she thinking about—she didn't *want* marriage, did she? Didn't want to be tied to one person and one place, obliged to follow one man for the rest of her life; putting him first even before herself. And in spite of the modern way of thinking, as far as she could see, that was still expected of wives. But deep down there was another reason why she would never love Richard in the romantic sense. There was no magic between them—no fireworks exploded when he kissed her. Although she refused to admit it, even to herself, only Gareth had evoked feelings like that. He had evoked a lot more besides, but she forced her mind away from that. It was uncharted territory and too disturbing to dwell on.

She found a space in the car park and drove into it. As she switched off the engine she heaved a sigh. Why couldn't life be as neat and tidy as one would like it to be? Why did the wrong people have to come along, disrupting everything—tearing all one's carefully laid plans to shreds? And what was she doing here—on her way to meet the one person responsible for the disruption? What was more to the point, why was her heart beating fast with anticipation?

Gareth was waiting for her in the lounge bar of the

Bunch of Grapes. It was a delightful old coaching inn in the centre of the town. He saw her first, as she stood in the doorway, scanning the crowded room. She had changed out of the jeans she had worn at breakfast into a tweed suit in soft shades of violet blue, with a silk shirt to match, and as she stood there, the light burnishing her bright hair and her cheeks pink from the fresh air outside, he took in the picture she made appreciatively. When she caught sight of him her expression changed, and although she was completely unaware of it she failed to keep the brightness out of her eyes as she came towards him.

'Hello, I thought I might have to wait for you.'

He smiled and pulled out a bar stool for her. 'There seems to be a lull at the moment—before all the autumn coughs and sneezes begin; and this morning there were none of the usual Saturday morning emergencies—DIY accidents—thumbs crushed by hammers, ankles wrenched falling off ladders—that kind of thing.' He looked enquiringly at her. 'What can I get you?'

When the barman had served her sherry he turned to her again. 'Talking of DIY, there's something I'd like you to see after lunch.'

Meryl looked at him over the rim of her glass. 'Oh, what's that?'

He smiled. 'Wait and see. I think you'll be interested, though.'

They ate a pleasant lunch in the sunny, old-fashioned dining room. Gareth asked if she had cleared the misunderstanding with Richard, but she glossed over what had passed between them, unwilling to think about it too much. She hated the thought of Richard being hurt. Inside her there was a small ache when she thought about it—a regret for childhood days and things past.

As they came out on to the sunlit market square, crowded with Saturday afternoon shoppers, Gareth looked at her.

'Where did you leave your car?'

'On the all-day car park,' she told him. 'It should be all right there.'

He nodded. 'Good—come on, then.' He took her hand and led her to where his own car was parked at the rear of the inn. Getting in, she fastened her seat belt and soon they were heading out of the town into the country-side. At a sign that said 'Brimcott', Gareth turned the car off the main road, and they drove for about a mile down a narrow lane to emerge on to a delightful village green. He stopped outside the post office and turned to her.

'Do you know this place?'

She nodded. 'Slightly. Pretty, isn't it?'

'Delightful. Wait here a minute, will you?' He got out of the car and disappeared into the shop, reappearing a moment later with a key, bearing a large label. As he got back into the car he dropped it into her lap. Meryl looked at the label and read the words: 'Jasmine Villa.' She looked at him.

'Is this the house you started to tell me about last night?'

'Yes. It's rather intriguing. I'd appreciate a feminine point of view on it.'

'I'm afraid I don't know anything about property or building,' she told him. 'You should have asked Aunt Maggie's advice. She's the home-maker of the family.'

Gareth didn't look at her as he said: 'I wanted *your* advice, though. It isn't the technical side of things I'm curious about, I can get an expert to look into that for me. I want your reaction to the atmosphere.'

'What for—I mean, why me?'

He drew the car into the side of the lane and turned to her. 'Why do you ask so many questions? Why do you always have to have everything explained to you? Don't you ever do *anything* on impulse—play it by ear?'

She felt her cheeks colouring. 'I'm not sure that I trust impulses.'

He started the car again. 'You don't have to trust them, just have them—for today, at any rate.'

Jasmine Villa turned out to be a small square house built of split flint lovingly edged with rose-coloured brick. It stood on a corner at the junction of two lanes and had a sleepy, dreaming look. Meryl realised later that this was effected by the half-drawn blinds at the windows, giving the appearance of half-closed eyes. Gareth switched off the engine and looked at her.

'Well, what do you think so far?'

She looked thoughtfully at the house. It certainly was attractive, with its rose-coloured, pantiled roof and pretty overgrown garden. The front door was painted yellow and had a fan-shaped light above it; the rustic porch sported a purple clematis on one side and a pink rambler rose on the other.

'It looks fine from here,' she said guardedly. 'But is it for sale? There isn't a board.'

'The owner has gone abroad,' he told her. 'It's for sale with the entire contents—apparently she went in a hurry and didn't have time to sell her furniture. It would suit me very well.' He opened the car door. 'Anyway, come and look.'

Meryl got out and followed him up the flagstoned

path. The garden was a profusion of late colour, chrys-
anthemums, Michaelmas daisies and bright dahlias;
some late roses still bloomed, and she remarked on the
fact that it was sheltered. Gareth pointed to the wall that
enclosed the garden, built of flint and brick, like the
house.

'It's a sun-trap, a very pleasant spot, wouldn't you
say?' He unlocked the front door and they stepped into a
square hallway, carpeted in red. The doors on either side
were panelled and painted white. Gareth opened one
and they walked into a cheerful sitting room, furnished
in colourful chintzes. A window looked on to the garden
and opposite was an open stone fireplace.

'Can't you just see a welcoming log fire burning
there?' he asked.

As they went from room to room Meryl began to feel
quite envious. It was exactly the kind of house she had
always dreamed of owning herself. The kitchen was
modernised to just the right extent for convenience
while still retaining its old-fashioned charm; upstairs
were three bedrooms and a pretty bathroom, and the
whole was perfected by central heating served by a small
gas-fired boiler, discreetly concealed in one corner of the
kitchen.

She looked at him. 'It's almost too good to be true. Is
there a snag—is the price astronomical?'

Gareth shook his head. 'Very reasonable, I thought,
especially with all the contents. Do you think I could be
happy here?'

She shrugged. 'Well, it *is* rather big for one person
—and it is a fair distance from Millington. But you do
have a car and you seem more than capable of looking
after yourself—' She looked at him enquiringly. 'Were

you thinking of employing a housekeeper?'

He laughed. 'Good heavens, no! A cleaning woman twice a week would be perfectly adequate. I wouldn't want anyone bossing me about and tidying all my things so that I couldn't find anything.'

'Like a wife, you mean?'

'Ah, but then a wife would have other advantages to compensate for all that, wouldn't she?' His eyes twinkled and she turned away to look out of the window.

'You'd need a gardener too, by the look of it.'

He joined her. 'Mmm, you're right there. I'd like to have a go at it myself, if only I had the time. My father would be in his element here.'

She turned to look at him. 'You've never spoken about him—or about your life before you came here.'

'I didn't know you were interested.'

She shrugged. 'I told you all about me.'

He crossed the room to sit down in one of the chairs. 'There isn't a lot to tell. My father and I have been on our own for some time. My mother left when I was still at school. She remarried soon after and lives abroad now, so I haven't seen her for years. Dad was a mining engineer until he retired three years ago. Until then he always kept the home going. When I was there we shared the chores, took care of each other, but when he retired he decided to move. I think he got it into his head that he was becoming a burden to me.'

Meryl perched on the arm of the settee, looking at him thoughtfully. 'Now I understand why you're so domesticated.'

He smiled. 'I'd prefer to call it self-sufficient. It's the way I grew up.'

'Is your father bitter—about women, I mean?' she asked.

He looked at her in surprise. 'Good lord, no! His own marriage failing hasn't turned him against it. He's still an idealist—a bit of a dreamer. I think he believes I should marry—but that I won't if I have him to think of. That's why he decided to go and live on his own.'

'Isn't it a coincidence, Aunt Maggie knowing him?'

He stared at her. 'I didn't know she did.'

'You mean she didn't tell you? She knew him when they were both at university, years ago. I found out through Libby.'

'That explains a lot,' he said thoughtfully. 'I thought some of the questions she asked me were rather irrelevant. Well, well!'

'Better not say I told you,' Meryl said quickly. She looked round. 'So—will you buy this?'

Gareth stood up. 'Do you think I should?'

'Surely the decision is yours. Why is it important what I think?' she turned to find herself facing him, and caught her breath at the look in his eyes.

'I thought you might like to spend some time here too,' he said softly.

'Me—but why?'

He smiled wryly, reaching out to touch her hair. 'Let's not play games with each other, Meryl. I told you I couldn't embark on a relationship with you at the beach house. Here, it would be different.'

She stared up at him. 'Are you asking me to—to—?' But she got no further; catching her to him, Gareth kissed her hard until she was too breathless to speak.

'You say you have no intention of marrying,' he said softly. 'I respect that choice—understand it, but surely even you can't deny that there's a strong attraction between us.'

She tried to speak, but somehow the words wouldn't come. He slid the jacket from her shoulders and down her arms, tossing it on to a chair, then he led her to the settee and sat down, pulling her down beside him. Cradling her against his chest, he kissed her again. She felt one hand unfastening the buttons of her shirt, but she was powerless to do anything about it. As his cool hand made contact with her skin her whole body tingled and she reached up to wind her arms around his neck. His lips caressed her ear, the line of her jaw—continuing down her neck to her shoulder and beyond, making her senses spin with delicious sensation. As he shifted his position to unfasten her bra she made a murmur of protest, but his mouth claimed hers again, parting her lips with gentle insistence, exploring her mouth with an infinite sweetness that set her whole being alight with longing. She heard herself murmuring his name again and again. It was as though some force beyond her control possessed her—took control as his caresses inflamed her.

'Gareth—darling, darling—' Suddenly a sound cut into her consciousness. The doorbell was ringing. Her eyes opened wide and she pulled away from him. He looked at her.

'Damn! Who can that be?'

'Only one way to find out.' Meryl was tidying herself as fast as she could, her cheeks crimson. Suppose whoever it was had looked through the window first? She felt ashamed. It looked so bad. It was still someone else's house, after all.

Gareth went into the hall and opened the front door.

She heard a woman's voice:

'I wondered if you'd finished looking round. I usually accompany people—the key—another prospective buyer—'

Gareth's voice was firm as he replied: 'I've decided to take it. I shall be contacting the agent first thing on Monday morning.'

A moment later he appeared in the doorway, a smile on his face. 'It was the postmistress. I think she was afraid we might run off with the contents! I told her we'd drop the key in when we'd finished looking round.' He crossed the room to her. 'Now, where were we?' He reached out for her, but she backed away.

'I think we should be going now. I forgot—I have to see someone this evening.'

He looked at her, frowning slightly. 'If I didn't know you better I'd say you were afraid.' She shook her head in protest, but he went on: 'What is it you're afraid of, Meryl—me or yourself?'

'Don't be absurd!'

He looked into her eyes, his own dark and smouldering. 'Do you have any idea how irresistible you are when you look at me with that—tremulous look? Half of me wants to take care of you, cherish you—while the other half—'

Meryl pushed past him, her heart beating fast as she pulled on her jacket.

'I really *do* have to go, Gareth. If you wouldn't mind taking me back to the car park, so that I can get my car—' She looked at him apprehensively. His expression was hard to read—angry—thwarted? She bit her lip. Had she led him to believe—? Suddenly he grinned.

'All right, you win! Come on.'

As she followed him out to the car she knew the shattering feeling of anticlimax. Did he think her stupid and naïve? Had she smashed her carefully built sophisticated image and made herself appear immature? As she climbed into the car she glanced at his profile. It told her nothing.

Damn Jasmine Villa and its insidious illusion of security! Damn the postmistress! Damn Gareth, but most of all—damn her own inability to disguise her feelings! She was her own worst enemy!

CHAPTER EIGHT

As they drove Meryl's mind was racing. She had said she
had to see someone; that meant she would have to take
herself off somewhere for the evening. She couldn't go
back to the beach house—Gareth might go there himself! She thought of Richard, then pushed the thought
aside. She couldn't make a convenience of him; it wasn't
fair. She didn't want to go to Aunt Maggie's either; she
might ask awkward questions. She bit her lip. Why did
life have to be so complicated? Gareth didn't speak until
they arrived at the car park, then he switched off the
engine and turned to her.

'I suppose you wouldn't like to tell me what's wrong?'

She forced a laugh. 'Wrong? Nothing's wrong. I just
remembered—'

'You don't really have a date this evening, Meryl, do
you?'

His eyes were disarmingly direct as they looked into
hers. His face came closer as he leaned towards her, his
arm along the back of her seat. She could see the tiny
flecks of gold in the grey eyes, and her heartbeat began
to quicken as she edged away, the car door handle
pressing into her back.

'I—I *do*,' she told him breathlessly. She looked at her
watch. 'And I'll be late if I don't go soon.'

His eyes continued to bore into hers. 'What happened
to make you change your mind? Back at the house you
were so warm and responsive, then—quite suddenly—'

'I forgot myself. I was carried away momentarily,' she told him. 'I like to be in control and—and—'

'And it terrified you to find your emotions taking over?' Gareth supplied.

She swallowed hard, staring at him. He had an almost uncanny way of reading her mind, and she wasn't sure that she liked it. In fact she was sure she *didn't* like it! She reached behind her for the door handle.

'Look, I must go, Gareth. Thank you for the lunch —and thanks for showing me the house. I'm sure you'll be very happy there.'

His hand shot out to grasp her wrist. 'Wait a minute! I asked you a question earlier, at the house, Meryl. You haven't given me an answer yet.'

She moistened her dry lips. 'About spending some time there with you?'

He brushed her forehead with his lips. 'I think you know it was more than that,' he said softly.

His warm breath made her skin tingle and she bit her lip hard. 'I'll think about it,' she hedged. 'I don't know —and I *have* to go, Gareth.'

His hand slid round her neck, the fingers lacing possessively into her hair as he cradled her head. He kissed her lingeringly. When he released her his eyes were speculative as they looked down into hers. 'You'll come,' he predicted coolly. 'We both know you will. It seems a pity to waste time playing games—but if that's the way you want it, I can wait.' He leaned across to open the door for her. 'But don't leave it *too* long, Meryl. Even my patience has its limit! See you later. Have a nice evening.'

Sitting in her own car, she watched him drive away with a curious sense of loss. What did she do now?

Slowly she drove to the Centre and let herself in with her key. Perhaps there would be a local paper in the waiting room. She could see if there was anything decent on at the cinema, then have a wash and freshen up before she went.

She was in her room, looking through the paper at her desk, when she heard footsteps in the corridor outside, and a moment later a voice addressed her from the half-open door:

'Meryl! I wondered who it was moving about.'

Meryl looked up to see Jean Taggart standing there, a bulging holdall in her hand.

'Jean! What are you doing here on a Saturday evening?'

'Just collecting some bits and pieces of laundry and generally catching up,' Jean told her. 'Mike is on call, and you know what that means—cold supper snatched when and if possible!' She looked curiously at Meryl. 'Are you all right? You look a little flushed.'

Meryl folded the paper. There wasn't anything on she fancied. Anyway, she was too restless to sit still for two and a half hours. She turned to Jean. 'I suppose you wouldn't care to spend the evening with me, would you? I've had a rather traumatic day. Maybe we could go somewhere and eat.'

Jean stepped forward and took her arm. 'Come home with me. We'll have the place to ourselves. When Mike's on weekend call he usually spends the time between calls in his study, doing his paper work. It's the only chance he gets. We can shut ourselves away and attack the pile of salad I've made. What do you say?'

'Sounds marvellous!' Meryl locked her door and slipped the key into her bag.

They sat in the Taggarts' comfortable sitting room, trays on their laps, eating the delicious chicken salad Jean had prepared. As they ate they talked about work and the Wellford Centre, but as Jean poured coffee she looked at Meryl shrewdly.

'Well, you haven't told me what was so traumatic about your day. Want to talk about it?'

Meryl sighed. 'I only wish I didn't have to. I wish I could cope. I've always thought of myself as "in charge" —but now, suddenly—'

'Now suddenly you're in love.' Jean smiled. 'I must say it's time you realised it. Everyone else has known for ages.'

Meryl stared at her. 'Known? But how?'

'It's been something of a foregone conclusion that you and Richard would get together eventually,' Jean told her. 'Anyone with half an eye could see he was potty about you.'

Meryl groaned. 'Oh, don't! You're making it worse.'

Jean frowned. 'You mean—it isn't Richard?'

'I only wish it were. It's typical of me that I have to find myself falling for the wrong man,' Meryl complained. 'If I could only love Richard life would be so simple—as it is—'

'If it isn't Richard, who is it, then?' Jean interrupted.

Meryl sighed. 'Maybe I'd better start at the beginning. Not many people know that for the past few weeks I've been sharing the beach house with Gareth Owen-Thomas.' She glanced at the other woman. 'It was Aunt Maggie's idea. I was against it from the start. And we couldn't get along at all. I mean, turning me out of my flat didn't exactly endear him to me from the beginning. Everything was impossible—then suddenly—' she lifted her shoulders helplessly, lost for words. Jean smiled.

'So now the conflict has turned to something else. So what's wrong with that?'

'I've had to hurt Richard, for a start,' Meryl told her. 'He found out that Gareth was at the beach house quite by accident this morning and got the wrong impression. Things came to a head between us and I had to tell him I could never feel for him in that way.'

'And that was when you realised what you felt for Gareth?' asked Jean.

Meryl stared at her. 'Maybe—I just don't know. We had lunch together, then he took me to look at a house he's thinking of buying—at Brimcott.'

She glanced at Jean, who urged her: 'Yes—go on.'

'He—suggested that I—spend some time with him there.'

Jean looked at her enquiringly. 'So—?'

Meryl chewed her lip. 'You don't understand. Things —well—*developed* while we were there. When he said "spend some time with him"—'

'He meant he'd like you to share his new house with him?' Jean smiled. 'Was that so very wrong of him? It would give you a chance to find out whether your love for each other is real before you take the final step.'

Meryl shook her head impatiently. 'But it isn't *like* that at all. He talks of "relationships" and "being attracted". I can't help feeling that he views it as dispassionately as he would the buying of a new piece of household equipment!'

Jean laughed. 'Oh, surely not! I suppose what you're saying is that he hasn't told you he loves you?' Meryl coloured. 'Do you want him to? Do you love *him*?' Jean probed. 'Would you marry him if he asked you?'

Meryl shook her head in confusion.

'I've always said I didn't believe in marriage. I even told Gareth that. As for love, how does one know—for *sure*, I mean?' She looked at Jean. 'I know that when he kisses me I forget everything—that my heart turns over at the sight of him or the sound of his voice—that being close to him is almost more than I can bear—' She stopped, biting her lip. She hadn't meant to go quite so far—to reveal herself so blatantly. When she looked up she saw Jean's gentle smile.

'Oh, my dear,' she said softly, 'I'm afraid you *are* in love. Quite hopelessly, I'm afraid. What you're really saying is that you're afraid of getting hurt—afraid that Gareth mightn't feel as deeply you do?'

'His own parents' marriage failed,' Meryl told her. 'And Jane Pritchard told me that Gareth was engaged but his fiancée ditched him for someone higher up the professional ladder, so I suppose it isn't surprising if he's afraid of committing himself again.' She looked up. 'What shall I do, Jean?'

'Only you can really decide that, love. If I were in the same situation I think perhaps I'd take what I could get and hope for the best,' Jean said thoughtfully. 'Maybe after a while he'd find he couldn't get along without you.'

Meryl shook her head. 'I don't know—I just don't know.'

It was about half-past ten when Meryl arrived back at the beach house, and as she parked the car and walked the fifty yards to the house she shivered in the cold wind coming off the sea. The swim she had this morning would definitely be the last of the year, by the feel of it;

when winter set in on this coast it did so with a vengeance.

She let herself into the house with her key and went straight to the kitchen. She would make herself a hot drink and take it to bed with her. She needed to think, and bed was the best place for that. But as she opened the door she stopped short at the sound of a soprano voice singing. At the sink, back towards her, was a small, blonde figure wearing Meryl's apron and peeling potatoes. She turned as she heard the door open and smiled.

'Hello, you're back early. We didn't expect you yet. Would you like some egg and chips? I'm just making some.'

Meryl stared at Jane Pritchard in amazement. Gareth had obviously wasted no time in finding himself another diversion!

'No, thank you. I wouldn't like to be in the way,' she said icily. 'I was going to have an early night, anyway.' She turned, but found her way blocked by Gareth's broad figure. He smiled down at her calmly.

'Don't be anti-social, Meryl. Stay and eat with us. We've just got in from the cinema.'

'It was *such* a good film, Meryl. You would have enjoyed it,' said Jane as she lit the gas under the chip pan.

Meryl bristled. Really! You'd think she owned the place! So they had been to the cinema? What a good job she had decided not to go; it would have been too humiliating if Gareth had seen her there alone.

'I'm afraid I shall have to ask you to excuse me,' she said. 'I have a headache. Goodbye, Jane.'

'Tell you what—as it's Sunday tomorrow why don't

you have a lie-in? I'll bring you your breakfast in bed if you like,' offered Jane.

Meryl turned to stare at her, then back at Gareth, who was leaning against the doorjamb. Seeing that she was waiting for an explanation from him, he straightened up, clearing his throat.

'Jane is your aunt's new tenant here,' he told her. 'As from tonight.'

Meryl swallowed hard. 'I see—and whose idea was that?'

Unconcerned, Jane took the eggs from the fridge and cracked two neatly into the pan. She turned to look enquiringly at Meryl, seemingly quite unaware of the tension that was building.

'Are you sure you won't have some?' she asked. Meryl shook her head impatiently.

'I happened to run into Jane this evening,' Gareth explained. 'She mentioned that she still hadn't found anywhere to live. I had to ring your aunt to give her my notice, so I suggested that Jane might take my place. I'm sure you two girls will get along like a house on fire.'

Meryl went into the sitting room without another word. She couldn't trust herself to say any more. Why did everyone think they could take her reactions for granted? She felt sure that sharing with Jane would be a disaster. Aunt Maggie really had gone too far this time. As for Gareth—!

He had followed her into the room and she turned to face him. 'What's the idea? Why did you do it?' she demanded.

He looked surprised. 'Jane really was getting desperate. And there is a room going begging here.'

'This is the second tenant I've had foisted on me,' she

said angrily. 'I shall soon begin to think everyone is conspiring to squeeze me out of the place!'

He took a step towards her. 'There *is* an alternative. You can always come to Jasmine Villa.'

She felt a lump rise in her throat at the mocking note in his voice. 'Perhaps you should ask Jane to share it with you,' she said bitterly. 'I'm sure you'd have no trouble persuading *her*!'

He took her by the shoulders. 'I suppose you know that you're behaving like a spoilt child again?' His eyes were granite-hard as they glared down at her. 'If you really want to know why I brought Jane back here tonight, it was because I knew I couldn't spend another night here alone with you without—'

'*Supper's ready!*' Jane's voice cut shrilly through his words, breaking the tension. Meryl shook Gareth's hands from her shoulders and walked out of the room. At the foot of the stairs she turned to look at him.

'Enjoy your supper,' she said coldly. 'Good night.'

Monday saw the beginning of a spate of high winds. From her window Meryl watched the sea heaving and tossing. All night long the sound of its fury had invaded her dreams. White-capped waves pounded the shore and the tide was extra high. As the three ate breakfast in the kitchen Jane expressed alarm.

'Is it *always* like this here? I'm not at all sure I can stand it,' she said nervously.

'Really? What a shame. I quite enjoy living dangerously,' Meryl said perversely.

Gareth shot her a warning look. 'It's quite safe,' he promised Jane. 'The sea defences are extremely strong. You remember, I showed you yesterday where the wall was built after the devastating floods of the fifties.'

'Yes,' Jane simpered at him. 'I must say I did so enjoy our walk yesterday afternoon, Gareth.' She looked at Meryl. 'You really should have come with us. We had a lovely time. We stopped for tea at that little place on the coast road—hot toasted muffins with lashings of jam and cream cakes to follow. Absolute death to slimming!'

Gareth laughed. 'A good thing you don't have to worry about things like that, isn't it?'

Meryl bit back a cutting remark as she got up from the table. 'I must go—my first call is at the hospital this morning. I'll see you later—'bye!'

As she collected her things she reflected that another week of this and she would go stark raving mad. Jane had announced that she would take over the cooking. She had rearranged the furniture in the sitting room, reorganised the kitchen cupboards and posted up a bathroom rota at the foot of the stairs. And so far she had only been in the house one day! It was like living in an institution!

Meryl closed the front door behind her and walked to the garage, head bowed against the gale-force wind. She would have to start looking for a flat of her own, though heaven knew where she would find one.

At St Luke's she found Sister Davies on Men's Medical in an imperious mood.

'It's your patient, Mr Johnson,' she told Meryl. 'He spoke his first few words yesterday—while his wife was here. And you'll never guess what the latest is. She asked to see me—complained that his Lancashire accent was back—seemed to think it was our fault!'

Meryl sighed. 'Oh dear. That happens sometimes —accents people got rid of years ago reappear when the speech returns. Surely she can't complain? The fact that he's speaking at all—!'

Sister's eyebrows rose. 'Just you try telling her that! I did, and I wasn't thanked for my trouble.'

Meryl found Mr Johnson looking glum. He didn't respond in his usual enthusiastic way to the exercises she gave him. At last she decided to call it a day and have a little talk with him instead—try to find out what was troubling him. She sat on the edge of his bed.

'There's something wrong, isn't there, Mr Johnson? Sister says you managed a few words yesterday. Won't you try for me?'

He shook his head.

'Is it because your voice sounded—different from the way you thought it would?'

He nodded unhappily.

Meryl took his hand. 'You know, it's like a new beginning—all the things you learned before have to be learned again. It may seem like a mammoth task, over-whelming at times, but try to look on it as a challenge. I know your wife wants to help. Perhaps, like you, she expects a little too much.'

He looked at her and nodded. Inwardly Meryl nursed angry thoughts about Mrs Johnson and made a mental note to visit her again. Why couldn't the woman see that her husband was doing his best? For a woman who wanted to help she was making a good job of discouraging him!

At St Winifred's the children were restless.

'It's the weather,' Mrs Venables told her. 'I've often noticed that stormy weather upsets them. I must admit that I hate gales myself.'

Meryl let them play at 'shops'. She had found it helpful for the older children who would soon have to begin the hazardous business of going out into the world. For such children the everyday task of asking for things they needed in shops could be frustrating and embarrassing. Meryl encouraged them all she could by the game she had devised, and found that gradually they became less tongue-tied and more fluent.

She had noticed that little Peter Sopwith had started at the school, and before she left she asked Mrs Venables how he was getting on. The headmistress smiled.

'He's a nice little boy, too bright to be here. I'm afraid it will hold him back.'

'He was held up at his other school because the other children teased him,' Meryl reminded her. 'Perhaps the answer is extra coaching at home. Does he mix with the other children?'

Mrs Venables shook her head. 'I wish he would. But he seems to prefer the company of older people—and he never stops drawing those pictures of his.'

'Did you save them for me?' asked Meryl.

Mrs Venables went to her desk and took out a bundle of childish drawings. 'Here they are. Some of them look quite violent—quite unlike Peter himself.' She shook her head. 'We never know what's going on in their little heads, do we? If we did, our job would be much simpler.'

Meryl tucked the drawings safely away and pulled on her coat, making a mental note to look at them later.

During the lunch hour she managed to track her aunt down. Tapping on the door of her surgery, she found her gathering her things together and asked if she had a minute to spare. Dr Margaret looked doubtful.

'I was going to rush home for lunch. It's ante-natal clinic this afternoon,' she said. 'I have a couple of house calls to make too. Two of my mothers went home this morning and I'd like to make sure they've settled in all right.'

'This won't take a minute,' Meryl told her determinedly, sitting down on the other side of the desk. Dr Margaret sighed and sat down again.

'All right, dear, but do make it snappy.'

Meryl came straight to the point. 'I really do wish you'd consult me before agreeing to take new tenants,' she said crossly. 'It was a big enough shock when I found myself sharing with Gareth—Jane Pritchard is about the last straw!'

'I thought perhaps you and Gareth had talked it over. Anyway, I'm sure you'll get along well enough,' Margaret said coolly.

'She's the organising type,' Meryl complained. 'She'll drive me mad if I have to put up with it for long! I'd be grateful if you'd make it clear that it's only temporary.'

Margaret pursed her lips. 'Why don't you tell her yourself?'

'I don't see why I should have to,' Meryl argued. 'After all, I didn't ask her to come, did I?'

'I don't think it's a good idea for it to be a permanent arrangement for any of you,' said Margaret. 'Gareth seems to have found himself a nice house, I'm sure you could find somewhere too.'

'I couldn't afford a place like Jasmine Villa, much as I'd like to,' Meryl said, then bit her lip as her aunt looked up sharply.

'Oh, you've seen it, then? Did he take you out there?'

'He wanted my opinion,' Meryl admitted reluctantly.

Margaret smiled. 'I see. I'm glad you seem to be hitting it off better. Of course, it will be some time before Gareth is ready to move, but I don't think you'll be too cramped at the beach house till he does.' She got up from her desk and began to put on her coat. 'Now I'm afraid you'll have to excuse me, dear. I really do have to run.'

When she got home that evening Meryl made herself a meal and ate before the others came in. When she arrived Jane was clearly thwarted.

'Oh, you've had yours,' she said from the kitchen doorway as she watched Meryl wash up her dishes. 'I thought we'd all eat together, the three of us.' She held out a loaded shopping basket. 'I went shopping in the lunch hour. I've got liver and onions.'

'Oh, what a pity!' said Meryl. 'I'm sure you won't mind if I leave you to share it with Gareth. I've got a case to study, so I shall be spending the evening in my room.'

On her way through the hall Gareth came out of the living room and grabbed her arm as she passed, pulling her into the room and closing the door.

'Do you *have* to be quite so bitchy?' he demanded angrily. 'The girl is trying to do her best. Why can't you meet her halfway?'

'I'm leaving that to you!' she told him pointedly.

'What's this case you have to study?' he asked.

'I've got some more of Peter Sopwith's drawings. Mrs Venables gave them to me this morning.'

'I see.' He relaxed a little. 'As a matter of fact I saw Peter this evening. His mother brought him along. He has a persistent cough, and it looks suspiciously like asthma.'

'Of the nervous type?' Meryl forgot her previous annoyance as Gareth nodded.

'I'm pretty sure it is, yes. I still think it almost certainly has something to do with the parents splitting up. Perhaps we could compare notes some time?'

Meryl nodded. 'Of course. It seems such a pity.' For a moment they stood looking at each other, then Gareth said:

'I made an offer for Jasmine Villa this morning, and the agent seems pretty sure it'll be acceptable to the owner. I should be able to move in as soon as I've signed the contract.'

Her eyes slid away from his. 'That's good.'

'Have you thought any more about what I asked you?'

Gareth reached out to cup her chin, lifting her face so that she could not avoid his eyes. Suddenly her mouth was dry.

'I—I can't—I mean, I need more time to think,' she stammered.

His eyes clouded as they looked searchingly into hers. 'Are you playing hard to get, Meryl? Because that's a game I don't participate in.' His fingers were hard as they slid round to the back of her neck, holding her fast, drawing her towards him. 'I'll tell you what: When you've made up your mind to come to me, *you* tell *me*. I'll wait to hear your decision.' He bent and kissed her hard. 'But as I told you before, don't leave it too long.' He stepped back and opened the door. Jane's shrill soprano could be heard warbling 'The Ash Grove.' Gareth smiled.

'I'll go and see if Jane needs any help, I think. See you later. And don't forget what I said.'

Meryl stared at the closed door, angry frustration seething inside her. If he thought she would ever—*ever* ask him for anything, he had another think coming!

CHAPTER NINE

IT was later in the week when Jane came up with the idea for the dinner party. Meryl had just finished an early clinic at the Centre and was snatching a quick cup of coffee before going on to St Winifred's. Jane tapped briefly on her door and came in, closing it conspiratorially behind her.

'Have you got a minute, Meryl?' she said in a whisper.

Meryl looked surprised. 'Yes—why, is anything wrong?'

There was an air of suppressed excitement about the other girl as she shook her head.

'Not wrong, no. I've just made a discovery, that's all. Did you know it was Gareth's birthday next week?'

Meryl shook her head. 'No, I didn't.'

'Well, it is. I was in reception and Sandra happened to have his file out. I saw the date of birth: he'll be thirty-five on Friday week. I had no idea: why don't we give a dinner party for him at the beach house?'

Meryl stared at her. 'Well, I—'

'We could do the cooking between us—you could do the easy things if you're not up to anything fancy. We could share the cost. It could be our present to him. We could ask your aunt, the Taggarts, Richard—' Jane paused, frowning and counting on her fingers. 'That makes us a man short, though—I wonder—'

'Wait a minute,' Meryl put in. 'Is it wise? I mean, the

whole thing might embarrass him. Don't you think we ought to ask him first?'

Jane looked horrified. 'Oh, no! That would spoil the surprise.'

'But we wouldn't be able to make all the preparation without him getting wind of it, would we? And what if he arranges to go out that evening?'

Jane pursed her lips. 'Yes, I do see what you mean.' She considered for a moment, then her face brightened. 'I know—we'll tell him we have something planned and that he isn't to go out.' She looked at Meryl's still doubtful face. 'Oh, go on, Meryl. It would be such fun. You needn't do *any* of the cooking if you don't want to. You could do the shopping and the table—the flowers and so on.'

'As a matter of fact I'm rather a good cook. It's just that I never get the chance,' Meryl said cuttingly. 'Why everyone has to assume that I'm useless in the kitchen, I don't know!'

'Sorry, I didn't mean—' Jane coloured. 'It's just that you seem so—well—' She bit her lip as she searched for the words. 'So career-orientated—a bit of a feminist, I suppose.'

It was Meryl's turn to colour. 'Just because I happen to think men who can't do simple things for themselves are feeble it doesn't make me a militant feminist!' she retorted.

'I didn't say *militant*. All right, we'll share the cooking —work the menu out together. Oh, *do* say yes, Meryl! I'm sure Gareth would love it. It could be a sort of parting gesture too—with him leaving the beach house soon.'

There was something appealing about Jane's blue

eyes and Meryl relented. 'Oh, all right, then. We'll get together this evening, shall we?'

'Yes—and in the meantime we can both be thinking about the extra man we need. Perhaps you can think of someone.'

As Jane was whisking out of the room she almost collided with Dr Margaret coming in. The older woman smiled at her niece as she closed the door.

'Jane looks pleased about something. Are you settling down together?'

Meryl nodded. 'We get along well enough, I suppose.'

'She's very popular with the patients. Always so bright and cheerful.' Margaret sat down at Meryl's desk. 'Got a cup of that coffee for me? I'm too rushed to stop really—just off to the hospital, but I wanted a word with you. It concerns one of your patients.'

Meryl poured her aunt a cup of coffee and sat down opposite her. 'Oh yes—who?'

'Paul Dixon.' Margaret stirred her coffee thoughtfully. 'I had a visit from his wife the other afternoon. She's pregnant.'

Meryl stared at her aunt. 'Pregnant—Julie?—But—'

'Almost four months,' Margaret told her. 'She'd been pretty certain herself for some time. I think she'd been trying to ignore the symptoms—hoping they'd go away. I confirmed it for her—took a test, just to be sure. It's positive, of course. I rang her this morning.' She glanced at Meryl. 'It must have happened just before Paul's accident.'

'Oh dear,' Meryl sighed. 'Poor girl! It couldn't have come at a worse time.'

Margaret nodded. 'She didn't say a lot, but I rather gathered that things are not too rosy between them.'

'He's taken his disability hard,' Meryl told her. 'Although he's making good progress he can't come to terms with it and I'm afraid he rather takes it out on Julie. I don't know how she'll cope with a pregnancy and a baby.'

Margaret stood up, looking at her watch. 'Well, I thought I'd better tell you. Maybe there's something you can do to help. Talk to the girl. I think she needs a friend—someone of her own age. I must rush now.'

As she drained the last of her coffee Meryl said:

'Oh, by the way, Jane had the idea of giving Gareth a dinner party for his birthday at the end of next week —Friday. Would you be free?'

Margaret looked pleased. 'What a lovely idea! Yes, I'll be free. Are you going to do it yourselves?'

Meryl smiled. 'According to Jane, yes. She very kindly offered me the "easy things" to do. So that my meagre talents won't be too challenged, I suppose.'

Margaret gave her a rueful smile. 'Perhaps she thinks your "talents", as you call them, lie in other directions.'

On her way home that evening Meryl called on Mrs Johnson. The moment she opened the door it was clear that the older woman knew why she had come. Her manner was defensive as she ushered Meryl into the living room and sat on the edge on the chair opposite her.

'I've been expecting you all week,' she said. 'I know Sister Davies tells you every little thing that happens.'

'It is important for me to be kept informed,' Meryl told her. 'Sister isn't "telling tales", you know.'

The woman coloured, twisting her handkerchief in her hands. 'It's all right for outsiders,' she said defensively. 'It's not the same when it happens to you, you know. Looking at it from a medical point of view is quite different.'

'I just wanted to explain to you that it's something that often happens, this business of the speech patterns regressing. Your husband lost his accent before. He can do it again if it's so important.'

Mrs Johnson shook her head. 'It's all such an uphill struggle. Nothing will ever be the same—*ever*!'

Meryl sighed as she watched the older woman fighting back the tears. If only she could face the problem with the fortitude of her husband! Gently, she said: 'I know how you feel, really. But if you could just try to put yourself in your husband's position. He really has tried hard. He can't help what's happened, you know. Your reaction to his first few words must have been shattering.'

'I know.' The words were barely audible as the woman looked up at Meryl. 'I've learned a lot about myself over these last weeks,' she confessed. 'It isn't pleasant to face the fact that you're not the kind, compassionate person you thought yourself, you know. It's a shock to discover that you're selfish and a coward—that you care more than you should about what others think.' She swallowed hard. 'You think I'm shallow and useless, I expect. I wouldn't blame you either. As for Sister Davies—'

'I think you're honest—and a little too hard on yourself,' Meryl interrupted. 'You expect too much—both of yourself and of your husband. Look, he'll be coming home soon. In the meantime how would you like to fill your time by doing some voluntary work with the disabled? It might help to put things in perspective for you. I could arrange it for you.'

Mrs Johnson looked at her in horror. 'Oh, no! I couldn't. I've plenty to do here—getting the house ready for when Gerald comes home—besides, I'm not at all sure I could cope with that sort of thing.'

'Isn't it time you learned?' Meryl asked her gently. 'You said you'd learned some unpleasant truths about yourself. Why not see if there are some admirable things about your character you didn't know existed? You might get some pleasant surprises.'

Mrs Johnson looked abashed. 'You have more faith in me than I have myself,' she said quietly.

'But not more than you deserve, I'm sure,' Meryl told her.

The visit to Mrs Johnson had taken longer than Meryl had planned and when she got back to the beach house Jane was already in the kitchen. She was bubbling over with excitement.

'You'll never guess where Gareth and I are going tomorrow,' she told Meryl.

'In that case you'd better tell me, hadn't you?' Meryl took off her coat and turned to face Jane, waiting expectantly for the revelation.

'Well, this afternoon we had a visit from the resident nurse on the gas rig,' Jane told her. 'He's Canadian and his name is Carl Blake,' she smiled. 'Actually he's *rather* attractive. He asked us both to go over and look round tomorrow. He said he thought it might be a good idea in case we ever have to go in an emergency. We're going across by helicopter. Isn't it exciting?'

'Very,' said Meryl as she rolled up her sleeves and set about peeling potatoes for supper. Jane's enthusiasm seemed to have driven all thought of food from her mind. 'Have you had any more thoughts about the menu for Gareth's party?' she asked.

Jane nodded. 'Well, yes I have, actually. But I had another thought too: Why not ask Carl Blake to make up the number? He was saying how much he misses his medical friends over there on the rig.'

'I suppose we could,' Meryl said without enthusiasm. 'Ask him tomorrow if you like. I've asked Aunt Maggie, and she says she isn't doing anything that evening and she'd like to come.'

'Good.' Jane took a notebook out of her handbag. 'I've made a list. I'll just tick her name.' She perched on the corner of the table. 'Now, I thought we could have a cold starter, so that we can make it in advance and keep it in the fridge. Then we could have a roast—chicken perhaps, with several interesting vegetables—a choice of sweets—perhaps fresh fruit salad and something hot, then cheese and biscuits to finish up with.' She looked at Meryl expectantly. 'What do you think?'

'Sounds fine,' Meryl agreed. 'And I daresay we could do quite a lot of that in advance. The trouble is that surely Gareth is going to wonder what all that food is doing in the fridge.'

'Oh, we'll meet that hurdle when we come to it,' Jane said happily. The front door slammed and she held a finger to her lips. 'Sssh—that's him now. We'll talk about it later.'

Over supper Jane looked at Gareth. 'Oh, while I think of it, could you keep the evening free on Friday week?'

He looked up in surprise. 'I think so—why?'

'Wait and see,' Jane said archly.

'Have you heard any more about Jasmine Villa?'

asked Meryl quickly, changing the subject. Gareth nodded.

'Yes, as a matter of fact, I heard this afternoon from the agent to say that my offer has been accepted, so the sale can go ahead. I should be moving in a matter of weeks now. The owner has even given me permission to go in and do any decorating or gardening I might want to.'

'That's good.' She looked up and her eyes met his for a moment across the table. The same thought was in both minds until Jane broke the spell by saying:

'When am *I* going to get to see this famous house of yours?'

'Not till it's all ship-shape,' Gareth told her. 'I shall have to throw a housewarming. Maybe you can help me with advice on the food?'

Jane giggled and threw a sidelong glance at Meryl, who bit her lip. At the rate she was going Jane would give the whole game away long before a week on Friday!

It was several days before Meryl got a chance to see Julie Dixon on her own, and even then she had to scheme to manage it. When Paul came for his physio session with Jean Taggart Meryl contrived to be free and went out into the waiting room, where Julie sat thumbing uninterestedly through a magazine.

'Hello, I've got a few minutes to spare—why don't you come in and have a coffee with me?'

The other girl looked up. 'Oh, that would be nice—if you're sure. I know how little time you get.'

Meryl had the coffee already made and invited Julie to sit down opposite her. 'I won't pretend this is an impulse, Julie,' she said as she poured. 'I've been wanting to have a word with you for some time.'

Julie coloured. 'You've heard—about me, I mean. Your aunt asked if I'd mind you knowing, and I said no.' Her eyes filled with tears. 'It seems awful that the only person I can't tell is my husband, doesn't it?'

Meryl pushed the cup of hot coffee towards her. 'Drink that—you'll feel better. What are you going to do?'

'I don't know.' Julie shook her head. 'I've thought about having a termination—not telling Paul at all. But I don't see how I could. I'd have to leave him, and I wouldn't know how to lie to him about a thing like that.'

Meryl sighed. 'Surely you *must* discuss it with him. It's his child too.'

'It isn't easy to discuss things when the other person has to write everything down,' said Julie, biting her lip. 'I know this must sound awful, but sometimes I think Paul uses his disability as a sort of weapon.' She looked up at Meryl tearfully. 'It all seems so hopeless!'

Meryl shook her head. 'Don't be so sure. I have an idea this might just tip the balance. Paul hasn't been trying as hard as he should. This might give him back his self-esteem, make him see that life has something worthwhile to offer again. It would be something for him to work towards. It's worth thinking about, isn't it?' She looked at Julie closely. 'You do *want* the baby, don't you? I mean, what did you and Paul plan before the accident changed everything?'

'That's just it,' Julie confessed. 'We weren't going to have a family—at least, not for ages. That's why it's such a blow.'

Meryl got up and went round to lay a hand on Julie's shoulder. 'Try not to worry about it. And don't make any hasty decisions. I have a feeling it might be a blessing in disguise.'

On Friday evening Meryl had planned to leave early so that she could get ahead with the preparation for the party before Jane got in from evening surgery. She was just clearing her desk when there was a tap on the door and Gareth walked in.

'Have you got a minute?' he asked.

She looked at her watch. 'Well, not really.'

A flicker of annoyance crossed his face. 'Sit down, Meryl. This is important.' She did as he said. 'Have you seen Peter Sopwith lately?' he asked.

'Yes, but he doesn't seem to be making much progress,' she told him. 'It's almost as though he's shut up in a little world of his own.'

He nodded. 'I've had his mother in to see me this afternoon. Very wisely she came alone. It seems that Peter's asthma is getting worse, and he's started having nightmares too. I'm wondering if he's a case for the combined clinic. Do you know when the next one is?'

Meryl opened her desk diary. 'There's one in ten days' time,' she told him. He rose from his seat.

'Right, I'll get him an appointment. Perhaps you'd like to write a report on him?'

'Of course.'

He saw her glancing at her watch again. 'I'm sorry if I'm keeping you,' he said tetchily. 'Do you have a date or something?'

'No.' She glared up at him. 'There's something I promised to do.'

'Well, I mustn't be the cause of your breaking a promise, must I?' And with this acid remark he strode out of the room, letting the door swing to noisily behind him.

Before she could stop them, quick tears sprang to her eyes. Since Jane had joined them at the beach house she had had no close contact with Gareth at all. In fact he seemed to go out of his way to avoid her. Obviously it was a matter of indifference to him whether she was hurt by his action or not. No doubt he was used to the women in his life falling at his feet at an invitation such as the one he had issued to her on the day they had visited Jasmine Villa. Her refusal was something he would not forgive in a hurry. As for his suggestion that she should *ask* to be allowed to reconsider—he couldn't know her at all to make such a suggestion. And so the situation between them was stalemate, and likely to remain so. If only she didn't feel so shattered by the whole thing! If only there were someone she could turn to, as she had once turned to Richard in times of trouble. Gareth had even put an end to that!

At the beach house she prepared vegetables, laid the table, arranged flowers. She assembled the prawn cocktails from the ingredients Jane had left in the fridge and chopped fruit for the fresh fruit salad, pouring the syrup over it and setting it aside to chill. She had made a large apple pie the previous evening and she took it from the pantry. It would only need warming after the main course was taken from the oven. At last everything seemed ready, and she went up to her room to change. She chose a long black evening skirt and a top of deep violet blue. It had tiny cap sleeves and a pretty scalloped neckline which enhanced the flawlessness of her ivory skin. Brushing the thick auburn hair smooth, she pinned it into a topknot and completed her sophisticated look with a pair of jet earrings. She was just taking a last look in the mirror when there was a tap on the door and Jane put her head round it. She looked flustered.

'Sorry I'm so late. It would be a full surgery this evening of all evenings! It looks as though there's a 'flu epidemic on the way.' She stared at Meryl. 'Gosh, you look fantastic! I'll never have time to make myself look as gorgeous as that.'

'Yes, you will,' Meryl told her. 'Everything's under control, and there's one thing—if *you're* late, most of the guests will be too. I'm all ready, so you can go and have a bath—take your time.'

Jane sighed with relief. 'Of course—you're right, everyone else will have to get ready too, won't they? I hadn't thought of that! Gareth's been called out, by the way, so I hope he isn't too long.' She smiled. 'You know, Meryl, when I first came here I thought you and I weren't going to hit it off, but we seem to be shaking down nicely now, don't we?'

Meryl grinned. 'Just go and get ready. There are still some jobs for you to do, you know. I haven't let you off everything!'

When the other girl had gone she had to admit to herself with a feeling of surprise that she was actually getting to like Jane—regarding her as a friend in spite of their differing personalities.

The first guest to arrive was Aunt Maggie. Meryl gave her a sherry, but there was hardly time to drink it before the Taggarts arrived with Richard. Jane appeared looking fresh and pretty in a dress of dark blue with a swirling chiffon skirt.

Meryl was in the kitchen checking the roast when the doorbell rang. Closing the oven door, she went to answer it and found a well built young man with copper-coloured hair standing on the step. He was holding a wrapped bottle.

'Hi there, I'm Carl Blake—Red to my friends.'

Meryl laughed and held out her hand. 'Snap! It's nice to meet another redhead. I'm Meryl Taylor. Do come in.'

Carl held out the bottle. 'I hope you won't be offended by this. No one said and I forgot to ask—so I thought I'd better bring one just to be on the safe side.'

Meryl took the bottle from him. 'There was no need, but thanks all the same. All contributions gratefully received, as they say.' She took his coat. 'Come into the sitting room and meet the others.'

They stood in the doorway and Meryl looked round. 'This is Carl Blake—he's resident nurse on the rig.' She looked at Carl. 'You know Jane, of course. I'll leave her to do the honours while I check the kitchen.'

As she closed the sitting room door she looked at her watch and wondered where Gareth was. Jane said he had been called out. She hoped he wouldn't be too long.

In the kitchen she strained the vegetables and turned the oven down low. Just as she was taking off her oven glove she heard the door open and looked up to see Gareth coming in. He stared at her, taking in her festive appearance.

'Hello—going out?'

She smiled. 'No, staying in, as a matter of fact. You're late.'

He ran a hand through his hair. 'I know. It was one of my elderly patients—pneumonia, I'm afraid. I had to get him into hospital.' He sniffed the air. 'Something smells appetising.'

'I hope it does. By the way, there are some people you know in the sitting room. Would you like to go in and have a drink with them while I dish up?'

He looked puzzled. 'People *I* know—are you sure?'

'To be honest with you, it's a little scheme Jane dreamed up for your birthday,' she told him. 'The meal is by way of a small present—from us both, and the people in the sitting room are your other colleagues.' She smiled. 'Jane would kill me for spoiling the surprise, but I thought I should warn you. These things can be a bit embarrassing.'

For a moment he looked taken aback, then his face broke into a smile. 'So this was what you meant when you said there was something you'd promised to do! How did anyone know it was my birthday? It's very good of you—but thanks for the warning all the same. I wouldn't have known what to say.'

Meryl put a tray of clean glasses into his hands. 'Here, you take this and we'll go in together.'

The meal was a great success. Meryl noticed that Richard hardly took his eyes off Jane all evening, and when she went into the kitchen later to make coffee he followed her on the pretext of 'helping'. Meryl was glad. It would be a relief not to have to feel guilty about Richard, and it was certainly time he started taking someone else out.

Everyone was interested in Carl's job on the rig and he was kept busy all evening answering questions. He told them that he had had previous experience of industrial nursing at home in Canada, and one glance at his husky frame showed that he had the necessary physical attributes for the job. Later, when they were relaxing with their coffee, he said to Meryl:

'You should come out some day and take a look round. The guys would like to meet you—they get very lonesome for female company.' He grinned disarmingly. 'That goes for me too.'

'I'd find it interesting, I'm sure,' Meryl told him. 'Jane was full of it when she came back the other day, especially the helicopter ride. It must be a rather spartan way of life out there.'

'It is,' Carl told her. 'But they look after us well. The food takes a lot of beating and the quarters are comfortable, even if they are a little small. The worst part is the monotony. But the men who work on the production platform only work for seven days at a time. It's enough, I can tell you. No smoking and no alcohol allowed, and of course we have all nationalities, so sometimes communication is difficult on a close basis. Tempers can flare in conditions like that, and you can't take risks with twenty-five million pounds' worth of steel island and equipment!'

While they were talking Meryl noticed Gareth staring at her once or twice as he sat talking with her aunt, but when he saw her looking at him his eyes shifted away. Carl chatted on, telling Meryl about the kind of accidents he had had to deal with—men being swept off deck in stormy conditions, crushed by the huge hawsers or felled by pieces of equipment. The divers too, he told her, led hazardous lives, with constant danger of dangerous gases being absorbed into their blood. Meryl found it all fascinating, and at last Carl said:

'Look, next time I get shore leave perhaps we could get together, Meryl. I haven't really had a chance to explore the countryside. I could hire a car and you could show me some of the sights.'

She laughed. 'I'd like that, Red, though I think you'll find East Anglia rather tame after Canada.'

'Not with a companion like you!' His hazel eyes laughed into hers. Suddenly Gareth appeared at her elbow. His hand closed around her arm in a proprietorial way as he said:

'I think your aunt wants to leave now, Meryl. Perhaps you'll get her coat for her.'

When she looked up into his eyes she saw that they held the cold enigmatic look that was becoming all too familiar, and it was only later, when all the guests had departed, that she discovered why.

She was in the kitchen, stacking the dirty dishes ready for washing-up, when he came in and closed the door behind him.

'Where's Jane?' he asked.

'I sent her to bed. She looked so tired, I'm afraid she might be going down with something.' She turned to look at him. 'If you want something to do you could give me a hand. It'll be midnight before I see my bed at this rate.'

Without a word he picked up a tea-cloth and began to dry. For a moment they worked in silence, then she said:

'You were rather rude—interrupting while Carl Blake was talking to me.'

Gareth snorted. 'I thought I was rescuing you. He'd been bending your ear all evening. People were beginning to notice.'

She turned to him, eyebrows raised. 'So—? I fail to see why it should worry you. As a matter of fact I found him very interesting.'

'So I noticed,' he said sarcastically. 'I thought it was

about time you gave some of your attention to your other guests.'

Meryl glared at him. 'And who do you think *you* are to tell me how I should divide my attention?'

He shrugged. 'If you want to know, I was embarrassed for you. It was almost pathetic, the way you were hanging on his every word! I broke it up for your sake more than any one else's.'

Meryl was so angry she couldn't trust herself to speak. With much clattering she finished the washing-up, pulled off her apron and rubber gloves and walked out of the kitchen.

Closing the door of her bedroom, she leaned against it, biting her lip in anguish. So much for the 'birthday treat'! How *could* she have fallen in love with someone as rude and overbearing as Gareth Owen-Thomas? If he behaved like this now what on earth would it be like to be married to him? But then marriage wasn't what he had in mind, was it?

It was a long time before she slept; her mind was too busy seething with fury over Gareth's boorish behaviour. The sooner he moved into his own house, the better. She wouldn't care if she never saw him again!

CHAPTER TEN

On Sunday morning Meryl woke to find the sun streaming through her window. It was one of those rare early winter days when nature seems to be taking a holiday. In the kitchen she found Gareth ready dressed in jeans and a thick sweater, finishing a hearty breakfast of bacon and eggs. He looked up as she came in with the papers.

'Good morning. What a day! I thought I'd drive over to Brimcott and tackle the garden. I bought some bulbs the other day and I really should get them planted.' He looked at her. 'Want to come and give me a hand?'

She stared at him. 'You're joking!'

'I'm not. I could do with the help and you could do with the exercise and fresh air—unless you have something else planned, that is?'

She shook her head. 'Well—I was going to have a lazy day.'

'Right, that's settled, then.' He rose from the table and carried his dishes to the sink. 'Hurry up and get ready. I'll wait for you. Put on your oldest clothes and some wellingtons if you've got some.'

'Wait a minute. Where's Jane?' asked Meryl.

He shook his head. 'I don't know. I thought perhaps she was having a lie-in.'

'I'd better check,' she said. 'She hasn't seemed very well for the past couple of days.'

She went through to the hall and tapped on Jane's door. A weak voice called out:

151

'Come in.'

Jane was still in bed. Her face was flushed and her blue eyes were heavy and dull. When she saw Meryl she shook her head.

'Don't come too near,' she said thickly. 'I think it must be 'flu. I feel terrible!'

Ignoring the warning, Meryl went over to the bed and placed a hand on Jane's brow. It was hot. 'You've got a temperature, by the look of you. Have you had a restless night?'

Jane nodded. 'I hardly slept at all.'

Meryl took the quilt off the bed and pulled up a chair. 'Here, wrap yourself in this while I make your bed. I'll bring you a hot drink and some aspirin.'

When she had made Jane more comfortable she went to the kitchen. Gareth looked at her as he put away the last of the dishes.

'You're not ready. What have you been doing?'

'I think you should take a look at Jane,' she told him. 'She has a temperature, by the look of her—'flu, I think. I'm making her a hot drink.'

Gareth went to look at the ailing girl, coming back a few minutes later to confirm that it certainly was 'flu.

'Looks like the virulent three-day type,' he announced. 'She should be all right if she rests and keeps warm.'

'I don't feel I can leave her,' said Meryl. 'Sorry about the gardening.'

He shook his head. 'Nonsense! She'll probably sleep for most of the day anyway. Tell you what—I'll ring Richard and ask him to keep an eye on her. I've a feeling it won't be too much of a chore to him!'

Meryl made sure that Jane was comfortable, then

changed into her oldest jeans and woollies. As they got into the car Gareth said:

'I was right about Richard. It's my guess he'll be at the house before we get to Brimcott!'

'He isn't on call, then?' Meryl asked.

He shook his head. 'It's your aunt's weekend.' He looked at her. 'Did you notice the way Richard was looking at Jane the other night?'

Meryl shrugged. 'You seem to be the one who picks up that kind of thing—and most of it's due to your over-active imagination!' Now that she had time to think she was asking herself what she was doing, meekly obeying Gareth's command to go and help him with his garden. Only the night before last he had been abominably rude to her, and now here she was doing exactly what he wanted again! She must need her head testing!

Jasmine Villa looked peaceful in the sunshine, but as they pushed open the gate and went in Meryl noticed that the garden really was neglected. Waist-high weeds filled the borders and the small front lawn was almost past mowing. She looked at Gareth.

'Going to have your work cut out, aren't you?'

He grinned. 'If you think this is bad you should see the back!'

He wasn't exaggerating. At the back the little walled garden was a mass of nettles and briar. Gareth rolled up his sleeves.

'I suggest we make a clearing here and maybe have a bonfire.'

An hour later Meryl's back ached; her hands were torn and bleeding from the vicious brambles and she felt hot and sticky. One hand in the small of her back, she straightened up and looked at Gareth.

'We should have brought a flask of coffee with us.'

'If you're thirsty we can pop down to the pub later,' he said without looking up. 'Silly to waste time now. Let's get on with it while the weather holds.'

It was half past twelve before he allowed her to stop work. The garden was looking much clearer and a huge pile of rubbish awaited burning. Gareth seemed untired and unruffled as he grinned at her.

'Okay, I think you deserve a break now.'

Meryl heaved a sigh of relief. 'Thank goodness!'

'Trouble with you town girls is that a little hard physical work makes mincemeat of you!' He threw an arm across her shoulders. 'Come on, the Rose and Crown is only a hundred yards down the road. We don't need the car.'

Meryl pushed a strand of hair out of her eyes. 'Can't I tidy up a little first? I must look a fright!'

He shook his head. 'Who's going to look at you anyway? You're fine. Come on. It'll be closing time by the time you've fiddled with your face!' His only concession was to allow her to wash her hands at the kitchen sink and run a comb through her tangled hair.

At the Rose and Crown they ate a ploughman's lunch, then returned to clear the front garden and plant the spring bulbs that Gareth had brought. It was dusk when at last he put a match to the bonfire. As they watched it flare up he slipped an arm around her shoulders.

'You've done well. Thanks for your help.'

Meryl sighed as she watched the sparks leap into the darkening sky. In spite of her aching back she felt fit and contented. It was a long time since she had spent a whole day in the open, and she had to admit that she had enjoyed it.

'I could do with a bath—I feel filthy!' she told him.

He laughed. 'Me too. I'm afraid we'll have to wait until we get back to the beach house, though—no hot water here as yet. The gas hasn't been turned on. And I'm afraid we'd better hang on for a bit to make sure the fire is safe.' He looked down at her. 'We can go inside if you like and sit down.'

In the tiny kitchen he studied her face, then, taking out his handkerchief, he moistened it at the tap and rubbed her cheek.

'You look like a Victorian street urchin,' he told her with a grin. 'Soot from the bonfire. There—that's better.' He pushed his handkerchief back into his pocket and gently brushed the hair back from her forehead.

'I don't know why I agreed to come with you today,' she told him. 'On Friday night you were horrible to me—and after Jane and I had slaved over the dinner party for your birthday too!'

He pulled a face. 'It was just that I didn't like to see you making a fool of yourself—and all for the sake of trying to make me jealous. It wasn't worth it.'

Her eyes blazed at him. 'And all for *what*? Making you jealous was the last thing on my mind. You really do have an outsized opinion of yourself, don't you? Didn't it occur to you that Carl Blake might be interesting to me in his own right?'

He shook his head at her. 'Oh, please, Meryl—let's not pretend.'

'As a matter of fact I find him *very* attractive,' she insisted. 'He's asked me to go out with him when he gets his next leave—so that I can show him around a little. I've said yes.'

'I know—I heard you saying it.'

'After all, you take other people out—there's absolutely no reason why I should refuse to go with Carl. He's a very nice person.'

Gareth smiled down at her, one eyebrow raised. 'Keep going and you'll convince yourself—if no one else!'

She coloured. 'You're quite insufferable!' She made to push past him, but his hands shot out to grasp her arms, holding her fast. She knew he was going to kiss her and she struggled to push him away, knowing deep inside that if he did she would be lost. His hand caught her chin, holding it in a firm grip as he pressed her back against the wall, holding her there with the weight of his body.

'Let me go—' she managed to gasp before his mouth covered hers. For a moment she remained stiff and unresponsive in his arms, but slowly the closeness of him, the pressure of his body against hers, the scent of him, smoky and earthy from the day's gardening, took possession of her senses. With a whimper she capitulated, relaxing against him, giving in to the pressure of his lips, allowing her mouth to melt into his while her heart raced within her.

When at last he relaxed his hold on her she hid her face against his shoulder, afraid to let him see what was in her eyes. He rubbed his cheek against her hair.

'Why do you fight me all the time, Meryl?' he whispered. 'Why can't you give in to the inevitable?' He held her a little away from him to look into her eyes. 'We don't have to hurry back, do we?'

'Jane—' she murmured, her heart thudding loudly in her chest. 'She might be worse.'

He shook his head. 'Richard will be looking after her.

Please stay, Meryl. You know you want to.'

'Who says I want to?' She looked up at him defiantly, but he smiled.

'Everything I'm holding here in my arms is telling me so,' he told her softly. His lips came down on hers again, taking her breath away, sending her senses spinning wildly. It was impossible not to respond to the urgency of his kisses. Every nerve in her body tingled with longing as they clung to each other. She could feel the strong beat of his heart against hers as he kissed her closed eyelids, her throat, pausing to whisper in her ear:

'Stay, Meryl—this time do what your heart is telling you.'

Suddenly she opened her eyes to see bright, vivid reflections dancing on the wall opposite. 'Gareth!' She pushed her hands against his imprisoning arms. 'Gareth—the *fire*! It's out of control!'

It was an hour later before they were able to leave Jasmine Villa. The dryness of the weather had made the rubbish tinder-dry, and although the fire had not actually been out of control as Meryl had first thought, it had certainly not been safe to leave. They had watched until the worst of it was over, then damped down the ashes with earth before leaving. In the car Gareth glanced at Meryl and laughed.

'I wish you could see yourself! You look like a chimney sweep.' He sniffed. 'And you smell like a kipper!'

She looked at him in disgust. 'Thanks for the compliment. That's what you get for helping a colleague out!'

'Colleague? Is that how you see me?' he smiled. 'You know, I'm still not sure which fire you were talking about when you said it was out of control! Perhaps you're unaware of how Freudian the remark was.'

Meryl ignored the implication. 'I rather suspect your motives in asking me to help you with the garden, anyway,' she said. 'For all you knew I might have been hopeless at gardening.'

'I asked you for several reasons,' he told her. 'First, I like your company. I find it stimulating.'

She laughed. 'Now who's being Freudian?'

'Actually it was your aunt's idea in the first place.'

She stopped laughing to stare at him. 'Aunt Maggie? You're joking!'

He shook his head. 'Not at all. I was telling her the other night at the party about the mess the garden was in, and she suggested that you might enjoy helping with it.'

Meryl was silent. Just what was Aunt Maggie playing at? Ever since Gareth had come to Millington she had gone out of her way to throw them together. Could she be matchmaking?

As they pulled up outside the beach house they saw Richard's car parked outside. Gareth looked at her.

'You get out here. I'll put the car away.' He grinned. 'You can have the bathroom first—but don't be all night about it!'

She got out and slammed the car door. 'I shall be as long as I like! I think I deserve a good long soak. And there isn't a thing you can do about it.'

He grinned. 'Don't be too sure—I'm an expert at picking locks! I'll give you fifteen minutes.' And with this he revved up the engine and drove off along the track in the direction of the garage.

Meryl found Richard in the sitting room, watching TV. He held a finger to his lips.

'Jane's asleep. Poor love, it really is a nasty attack of 'flu. I'm afraid she'll be out of action for a few days.'

Meryl pulled off her anorak. 'I hope you don't catch it.'

He shook his head. 'Don't worry, I had my anti-'flu shot weeks ago, like any responsible GP. Jane should have had one too, silly girl.' He looked her up and down. 'Good lord, you look terrible! What on earth have you been doing?'

She sighed. 'I allowed myself to be conned into helping Gareth with his new garden. We burned the rubbish and the fire got a bit fierce. We had to wait until it was safe. I'm dying for a bath. Be a love and put some coffee on, will you?'

She was just getting out of the bath when she heard the telephone ring. A moment later someone rattled the door handle.

'Meryl!' It was Gareth's voice. 'You'll have to come out and let me get cleaned up—it's an emergency!'

'Right.' She dried herself quickly and slipped into her dressing gown. She found him waiting outside the door. 'I've started to run the bath for you,' she told him, then stopped when she saw the look on his face. 'What is it? What's wrong?'

'I've got to go out to the rig,' he told her. 'That was a call from Blake. He has a badly injured man on his hands and he wants to get him into hospital as soon as possible. There'll be a helicopter to pick me up in fifteen minutes. The police have given it clearance to land on the sports field.'

'Anything I can do?' she asked.

He nodded. 'Yes. With Jane sick I need you to come with me. Get ready as quickly as you can, will you?'

She stared at him. '*Me?* But why? I mean, I'm not a nurse.'

'You know your first aid and you come from a medical family. Look, Meryl, he sounds pretty bad—a case for intensive care. Richard's alerting the hospital now. If he should go into cardiac arrest in the helicopter on the way over I'll need assistance. Just get ready, there's a good girl.'

The next minutes were a blur of feverish activity. Gareth hastily washed and they drank the coffee Richard had made them, then they were in the car again and on their way. As they drove Meryl asked for the first time:

'What happened—was there an accident?'

Gareth was driving fast, his eyes concentrating on the road. 'It seems as anchor wire snapped. The man not only received a bad head injury but fell overboard as well. It was lucky they managed to get him out before he drowned.' His jaw set firmly. 'I only hope we can save him.'

Meryl's heart quickened. It was a big responsibility. She hoped she could live up to Gareth's confidence in her.

On the sports field they waited for the helicopter to land. They did not have long to wait. As they climbed in the pilot greeted them:

'Hello there. Belt yourselves in and we'll take off at once. You'll find some protective clothing back there —you can get into it later.'

He was right. Thick waterproof overalls had been

supplied, and bright orange hard hats, which they proceeded to put on.

In minutes they were airborne, the sea below them, and it wasn't long before they could see the lights of the rig below, looking like a jewelled ornament on black satin. The helicopter began to lose height and soon they could make out the bold circles painted on the helicopter pad in the centre of the drilling platform. Another few minutes and they were landing, the helicopter's blades whipping the air above them as they slowed and stopped. Meryl and Gareth struggled into the overalls. Meryl's were far too big and she had to roll up the arms and legs. Gareth grinned at her wryly as he bent to adjust the strap of her hard hat.

'You'll do,' he said briefly.

Carl Blake was there to meet them as they stepped out of the craft, his freckled face relieved.

'Good of you to make it so quickly. I've got the man below in the mess room, it was the most accessible place.'

As they followed him Meryl looked around her. Out here the wind was like a gale, cutting and bitterly cold. She shuddered as she imagined falling into the icy, heaving waters below, especially with a head injury. Gareth held her arm fast as they made their way across the slippery decks.

They found the man unconscious, and Gareth made a brief examination. 'He may have a skull fracture,' he said. 'He's certainly in severe shock. If it weren't for the circumstances I wouldn't move him—as it is—' He straightened up and looked at Carl. 'Do you have an oxygen supply I can borrow in case of emergency?'

'Sure. I'll get one of the guys to load it for you. I'll get a stretcher too.'

'I'll need his papers,' Gareth said.

'I've got everything here.' Carl handed Meryl an envelope. She looked at him. 'What about the man's next of kin?' she asked. 'Is there anything I can do about notifying them?'

Carl shook his head. 'I've already looked into that. He has no family. The person he's named is a Mrs Marilyn Sopwith. She's a local girl he's planning to marry when her divorce comes through.'

Meryl caught her breath and looked at the name on the man's card: Frank Armstrong. This was the 'Frank' little Peter was always drawing in his pictures—his mother's boy-friend!

Carl hurried off to enlist the help of three brawny men, two to carry Frank on the stretcher while the other loaded the emergency resuscitation equipment on to the helicopter. Meryl helped Gareth to wrap the man in plenty of blankets and a few minutes later they were taking off again, calling goodbye to Carl above the ear-splitting noise of the rotor-blades.

Gareth sat close to the man in the helicopter, checking his pulse and respiration every few minutes. Meryl looked at him.

'How bad is he?'

He shook his head. 'Not good. The shock is the worst aspect of his condition. His pulse is very weak. I can hardly feel it—' He broke off, dropping the man's wrist and moving his fingers to the carotid artery in his neck. Leaning over, he pulled aside the blankets and pressed an ear to his chest. 'My God, he's stopped breathing! Quick, Meryl, help me!'

Propping a rolled blanket under the man's shoulders, he tilted his head back and began to breathe into his lungs, pausing to shout at Meryl: 'Massage his heart. You know how.'

Meryl located the base of the breastbone and applied the heel of her hand to the spot, applying rhythmic pressure with the other hand. They worked for a few minutes, then Gareth looked up.

'You take over here while I do that.'

Her own heart thumping, Meryl moved to the man's head, then, pinching his nostrils as Gareth had done, she took a deep breath and forced it steadily into the torpid lungs, willing the still heart to revive. Seconds later Gareth said:

'Okay, I think he's all right. You can stop. I'll get some oxygen into him. Cover him up again.'

As she watched, weak with relief, the colour came back into the man's waxen face and soon he was breathing oxygen through the mask Gareth held to his nose and mouth.

They landed in the grounds of Northwich General and within minutes the patient was rushed up to Intensive Care. Meryl waited while Gareth went up to the ward with him to consult with the doctor on duty. At last she looked up as she heard footsteps in the corridor and saw him coming towards her. He still wore the rig overalls and carried the hard hat under his arm. He looked tired and his jaw was dark with stubble. Meryl felt her heart stir within her. She stood up and went to meet him.

'Is he all right?'

He nodded. 'The consultant says he must have an iron skull—it's only a hairline fracture. As I said, it was

the shock that affected him so badly. He'll be fine.'
He slipped an arm around her shoulders. 'You did
marvellously. Thanks.'

They were brief words, but with the weight of his arm
around her shoulders, pressing her against him, she felt a
warm glow of satisfaction.

'I'd never done that before,' she told him, 'except on
the dummy in the classroom. It's very different—the
real thing. I'm so glad he's going to be all right.' She
swallowed hard. 'I could almost cry.'

Gareth grinned. 'Not here, if you don't mind!'

The helicopter set them down on Millington's sports
field again, and as they climbed wearily into Gareth's car
Meryl looked at her watch. It was three a.m. She sighed.
In four more hours it would be time to get up and get
ready for work. They drove in silence until they turned
off the coast road on to the track that led to the beach
house, then the car suddenly slowed and stopped. Meryl
looked enquiringly at Gareth.

'What's wrong? Why are we stopping?'

He gave her a wry smile. 'Would you believe I ran out
of petrol?'

She stared at him for a moment, then began to laugh.
'In the circumstances—yes, I would. Even you couldn't
time things as badly as that!' She peered out of the
window. 'Oh no! We're still at least a mile and a half
from the house.'

Gareth shifted in his seat. 'Well, I don't know about
you, but I'm staying right where I am. These seats
recline and there's a rug in the back. What do you say?'
When she didn't reply he pressed a button at the base of
the seat and the next moment she found herself lying
back in a prone position. Reaching into the back seat,

Gareth drew out a warm plaid rug and tucked it round her.

'You seem to have made up my mind for me,' she said wearily.

He bent and kissed her briefly, then slipped an arm round her and drew her head comfortably into the hollow of his shoulder. 'I'm beginning to realise I might have to do that more often in the future,' he told her. 'You know, I was wrong about you.'

She twisted her head to look up at him. 'How?'

'When I first met you I thought you were over-confident and too big for your boots,' he confessed. 'The orphaned waif, indulged and pampered by her doting grandfather and aunt. I thought you were spoiled and over-privileged, conceited and altogether unbearable.'

Meryl smiled sleepily. 'Thanks—I find your flattery overwhelming!'

'I was wrong, though,' he repeated. 'You've got guts —I like that in a woman. There's only one thing wrong with you—you can't trust your own instincts. That's why I say I shall have to help you make up your mind.' He kissed her, then leaned back with a sigh. 'You were right about one thing—I could have timed this better. The perfect setting for seduction and here we are, both of us, too weary for words. He cuddled her close. 'Good night, Meryl, *cariad*.'

Meryl's eyelids drooped. The car was warm and she felt a deep sense of contentment, snuggled cosily against Gareth's chest. It had been quite a day. She had learned a lot about herself—about Gareth too. She knew now beyond all doubt that she wanted to be with him—that she felt something deep for him. Conversations she had had with Jane and with Jean Taggart drifted through her mind. Gareth had been let down once, so he would be wary. It made sense to test what they felt to see if it really was love. She took a deep breath, then said:

'Gareth, about Jasmine Villa—about your suggestion that I should—well, spend some time there with you. I've made up my own mind about it. I *would* like to.'

When there was no reply she raised her head to look at him. He was fast asleep.

CHAPTER ELEVEN

MERYL sat at her desk, listening to the ringing of the number she had just dialled. She wasn't looking forward to the task ahead of her. There was a click at the other end and a woman's voice answered:

'Hello, Millington 4053. Marilyn Sopwith speaking.'

'Good morning, Mrs Sopwith. This is Meryl Taylor speaking. I have some news for you. Please don't be alarmed, but your friend Frank Armstrong is in Northwich General Hospital. There was an accident on the rig last night.'

'Oh no! What happened? How is he? Is it serious?'

'No. He had a very lucky escape,' Meryl told her. 'I've just rung to enquire and he's regained consciousness. He has a hairline fracture of the skull, but he isn't in any danger. You were down as his next of kin, so I promised I'd let you know.'

'Thank you.' Mrs Sopwith sounded shocked. 'I only saw him on Saturday. He was off all last week, you see.' There was a pause, then she said: 'As a matter of fact, I told him it was all off between us—because of Peter, you see. I'm pretty sure his trouble was because of Frank and me.'

Meryl sighed. 'I'm sorry to hear that. But you'll want to go and see him in the circumstances.'

'I don't know. I don't have any transport and the buses are so awkward—then there's Peter—'

'Look, I have to go over there this afternoon to take a

167

clinic,' Meryl told her. 'If you can be ready just after one o'clock I'll take you. I'm sure he'd appreciate it, Mrs Sopwith.'

'All right, I'll come. Thank you for your kindness, Miss Taylor. I'll see you at Wellford House at one o'clock, then.'

As Meryl replaced the receiver there was a tap on the door and her aunt walked in. She was wearing the white coat she always wore for her ante- and post-natal clinics. 'Hello, dear. I thought I'd just pop in and congratulate you for last night's brave effort. Gareth is full of praise for you. He's just been telling me about it.'

Meryl nodded. 'I've just been ringing the patient's next of kin. I said I would as it was someone I knew—the mother of a small patient of mine, as it happens. I'm taking her over to Northwich to see him this afternoon.'

'And I'm seeing the wife of another of your patients this morning,' Margaret told her. 'Julie Dixon. She's coming up to me while her husband is in your hands. I understand you had a talk with her the other day.'

'Yes. The poor girl was rather down. I gave her what advice I could, but there isn't a lot one can say without appearing to interfere, is there? Not being married myself I haven't the experience, anyway.'

Margaret smiled enigmatically. 'Ah well, perhaps one day—' She looked at Meryl speculatively. 'You look tired. You can't have had very much sleep last night.'

'No, I didn't.' Meryl got up and began to bustle round the room, making it ready for the morning's clinic. 'Jane seemed better this morning, by the way,' she remarked. 'I hear you managed to get a stand-in.'

'Yes, thank goodness. Do give her my love and tell her I hope she'll soon be fit again.' Margaret stood by the door, regarding Meryl. 'Did you give Gareth a hand with his garden yesterday, by the way?' she asked.

'Yes—and thank you for offering my services,' Meryl said dryly. 'Thanks to that I'm as stiff as a board this morning!'

Margaret smiled. 'I'm sure it was worth it,' she said mysteriously, but before Meryl had time to analyse the remark she had gone.

Actually she wasn't sure whether her stiffness could be attributed to the gardening or the remainder of the night spent in Gareth's car. Certainly this morning on waking she had felt terrible. She and Gareth had walked the mile and a half back to the beach house to bath and dress for morning surgery, with scarcely enough time to snatch a cup of coffee, let alone talk. Jane hadn't even missed them and Richard had left a note to say she was feeling a little better and that he had left at midnight. Meryl thought ruefully about the impulsive decision she had made, wondering what would have happened if Gareth had not been too sleepy to hear it. In the cold light of day it seemed hasty and reckless. Last night everything had been coloured by the excitement and drama of the occasion; perhaps it was just as well that Gareth had been too tired to stay awake.

When she saw Paul Dixon she was quite amazed at the difference in him. He looked brighter and much more cheerful, and when it came to the exercises she found that he had made great strides with his speech in the past week. Before he departed he passed her a note. Opening it, she read: 'I'm going to be a dad!'

She patted his arm. 'Congratulations, Paul. You'll really have to get your skates on now with your speech and your physio, won't you? There'll be lots to do.'

He nodded and grinned happily. A little later Julie popped her head round the door.

'Paul's waiting in the car, but I thought I must look in to thank you,' she said. 'I did as you said and told him. It's made all the difference. I think it's done something for his confidence—made him feel like a man again. He's full of plans. We're happier than we've been since his accident.'

'It was only an educated guess,' Meryl confessed. 'But I'm so glad it worked.'

She only had time to snatch a quick coffee and a sandwich at lunchtime, before getting ready to drive over to Northwich. True to her word, Marilyn Sopwith was waiting in reception as she came through. Meryl smiled.

'Thank you for being on time, Mrs Sopwith. My clinic is at two and I like to be there in time to sort through my notes and refresh my memory.'

As they walked out to the car park Meryl noticed that the other woman was pale and drawn, and when they were in the car she said:

'Please don't worry about Frank. He's going to be fine now. He's a very strong man, you know.'

Marilyn looked at her. 'I feel so bad about the accident. I can't help feeling that it might have been my fault. Maybe he wasn't concentrating as he should. We had a row, you see—about Peter. Frank said I shouldn't let him rule my life, but he's taken against Frank so much—having nightmares about him, and now these asthma attacks.' She glanced at Meryl. 'God knows I didn't want to have to choose between them, but what could I do? My own child had to come first.'

Meryl shook her head. 'You can rest assured that it

wasn't your fault. An anchor wire snapped, it hit Frank and swept him into the sea. It could have been nasty, but it was a pure accident, nothing to do with anyone.'

Marilyn sighed with relief. 'Thank God!'

'Have you told Peter?' Meryl asked. Marilyn shook her head.

'Not yet. I haven't had the chance. He's at school.' She sighed. 'I tried everything, you know, to get him to like Frank. I told him that Frank was like us—didn't have anyone, that we needed each other. Frank tried too—bent over backwards to please the boy, but nothing worked.' She looked at Meryl, her eyes full of tears. 'He's a good man, Miss Taylor. I'll never find anyone else like him.'

At the hospital Meryl went to Outpatients to take her clinic, promising to meet Marilyn again at four o'clock. When she came out into the car park she was waiting, looking happier than before. As they drove she kept glancing at Meryl; finally she seemed to make up her mind.

'The nurse in Intensive Care told me what you and Dr Owen-Thomas did last night,' she said. 'Frank owes you his life. I think it's wonderful.'

'I only did what I was told,' Meryl told her. 'It was a pure fluke that I was there at all. Our practice nurse was ill, so I went instead.' All the same, in spite of her protestations she felt a warm glow.

When she got home she found Jane in the kitchen preparing vegetables for supper.

'What do you think you're doing?' she admonished. 'I thought you were going to stay in bed.'

Jane shook her head. 'I feel so much better. I couldn't lie there doing nothing any longer. I've been enough trouble already. The least I could do was try to pull my weight again.'

'You certainly look better,' Meryl remarked. 'Gareth said it was probably a 'flu of the three-day variety.'

'I must have slept heavily last night,' said Jane. 'I didn't hear you and Gareth come in. Richard popped his head round the door and said good night—I think that was around twelve. I must have dropped off soon after that. I didn't hear you till this morning.'

Meryl looked at her for a moment, then gave her a rueful smile. 'You didn't hear us because we didn't come in,' she explained. 'Gareth ran out of petrol on the way back and we were too exhausted to face the walk. We spent the rest of the night—what was left of it—in the car. But that's between ourselves. I'd be grateful if you didn't mention it to anyone else, they might get the wrong idea.'

'I see—and would they be wrong?' Jane asked meaningly. 'It sounds very romantic.'

'They most certainly *would* be wrong,' Meryl told her. 'After all that had happened on the rig, plus a day's hard labour in the garden of Jasmine Villa, the last thing either of us was feeling was romantic!'

Jane frowned. 'I *would* have to go and miss a chance to take part in a dramatic rescue. Damn this 'flu!'

'It didn't feel dramatic at the time,' Meryl told her. 'Just terrifying—for me at any rate. And I think those men deserve every penny of what they earn out there on that rig. Actually, I've been to see the victim this afternoon.'

Jane looked up. 'Oh, really?'

'Yes, I didn't tell you that he happened to have a vague connection with a patient of mine, did I? He's a friend of little Peter Sopwith's mother. I gave her a lift over to Northwich to see him. The poor man hasn't any family, you see.'

When Gareth came in he looked tired, and soon after supper he was called out. He was gone some time and Meryl was in the kitchen doing some washing when he came in. He sat down at the table with a sigh and she looked at him sympathetically.

'Would you like me to make you a coffee.'

He nodded. 'Better make it a black one—I may be called out again. That was young Peter Sopwith with another of his asthma attacks. This one was quite spectacular.' He looked up at her. 'By the way, did you know that our patient last night was a friend of that family?'

'I kept meaning to mention it to you,' she told him. 'I took Mrs Sopwith over to Northwich General to see him this afternoon. They were planning to get married, but it seems that Peter couldn't take to him.'

Gareth pulled a wry face. 'I heard all about it from Mrs Sopwith. Kids! I had a word with the young man in question, and now that he knows about the accident it seems he's blaming himself. Remember all those drawings of the big man and the water with sharks? It was Peter's way of wishing something bad on his mother's new man friend.'

'Ah—and now he's feeling guilty? Poor Peter!'

'Poor Frank Armstrong, you mean!' protested Gareth. 'It seems that child has put those two through seven kinds of hell trying to figure out where they'd gone wrong. Now all the little monster wants is to have Frank back again!'

Meryl looked at him. 'Human beings are strange creatures sometimes, aren't they?'

'If you mean that we don't always know what we want—yes, you're right.' Meryl couldn't meet the dark eyes that looked at her so directly. She turned away as the kettle boiled, grateful for the diversion.

As Gareth took the cup from her he said: 'I haven't had the chance to tell you—my father is coming to pay me a visit. He telephoned the surgery this afternoon.'

Meryl smiled. 'Oh, how nice! He and Aunt Maggie will have a chance to renew their acquaintance.'

He stirred his cup thoughtfully. 'Yes. I tried to get him to put the visit off for a while, until I'd moved into Jasmine Villa. He could have stayed with me then, instead of having to put up at a hotel. But he wouldn't hear of it—said someone I know had offered to give him a lift.'

Meryl slid into the chair opposite with her own coffee. 'Oh? An old friend?' she enquired.

'I imagine so. I tried to get him to tell me who it was, but he wouldn't. He says it's to be a surprise.'

'Sounds exciting.'

Gareth pulled a wry face. 'I'm not sure that I like surprises.'

The telephone rang and he got up from the table. 'That will probably be Mrs Sopwith. I gave Peter an injection—a mild sedative, and I asked her to ring me and tell me how he was in an hour.'

When he came back into the room he looked more relaxed. 'Well, well. It seems that Peter wouldn't go to sleep until his mother promised to take him to see Frank tomorrow. I think he wants to make his peace. It looks as though that accident was the proverbial "ill wind".'

Meryl chewed her lip for a moment before she asked: 'Gareth, why did you ask *me* to go with you last night?'

'I told you. I had to have help and Jane was ill.'

'But Richard was here. Why didn't you ask him?'

He raised an eyebrow at her. 'Two doctors to attend to one injured man? Rather like cracking a peanut with a sledgehammer!'

She said no more, but she couldn't help feeling that she had been put through some kind of test, and she wasn't sure that she approved.

The last patient for afternoon surgery had just left on Friday afternoon and Meryl was in reception, checking her appointments with Sandra, when the door opened and a tall, grey-haired man walked in. Sandra gave him her brightest smile.

'Good afternoon. Can I help you?'

'I was looking for Dr Owen-Thomas,' the man said hesitantly. 'This is the Wellford Centre, isn't it?' His voice was soft with the merest trace of a Welsh accent.

'Oh, I'm sorry, afternoon surgery is over now.' Sandra told him. 'Would you like to make an appointment for tomorrow morning?' She drew the appointment book towards her, but Meryl stepped forward.

'I think there's a mistake, Sandra.' She looked at the man. 'Are you Mr Owen-Thomas—Doctor's father?'

He smiled, and she saw that he had the same clear grey eyes. 'That's very clever of you, Miss—Miss—'

'Taylor,' Meryl supplied. 'Meryl Taylor. I'm Dr Margaret Taylor's niece. I believe you know her?'

The handsome face broke into a smile, 'I do indeed —or rather I did many years ago. Is she still in practice? Is she well?'

'She is, and you must certainly meet. I'm sure she'll be delighted to see you again. If you come this way I'll take you to Gareth's surgery. I think he's still in the building.'

Mr Owen-Thomas hesitated. 'Well, actually I have someone with me—waiting in the car—'

'That's no problem. Sandra will go out and ask them to come in—won't you, Sandra? Please come this way.' Meryl led the way down the corridor to Gareth's surgery and tapped on the door. Hearing him call to her to enter, she opened it, holding it for Mr Owen-Thomas to go in, then she closed it discreetly behind her.

Going back to her room, she gathered up her things. She tidied the room and took a last look round before switching off the light, then she picked up her coat and came out into the corridor again.

In reception she stopped as a dark-haired, striking-looking woman got up from one of the chairs.

'Ah, could you tell me the way to Dr Owen-Thomas's room, please? Your receptionist is busy on the telephone.'

Meryl looked at the slim, elegantly groomed woman in her smart city clothes. She had certainly not seen her before. 'I'm sorry, but the doctor has someone with him at present,' she said. 'Are you a patient?'

The woman gave a tinkling laugh. 'Good heavens, no! Gareth and I are old friends—in fact we were almost married once. I'm Frances Graham. I drove his father here from Wales this afternoon.'

'Oh!' Meryl was taken aback. So this was the surprise Mr Owen-Thomas had spoken of! She wondered how Gareth would view it? Would he be pleased to see his ex-fiancée again? She managed a smile.

'I see. Of course. If you'd like to come this way—' For the second time she walked down the corridor towards Gareth's room and tapped on the door, but at that moment her aunt came out of the room on the opposite side of the corridor. She was carrying a thick folder.

'Oh, Meryl—there's something I have to check with Gareth—' She flashed a smile at the elegant woman with her niece. 'I'm sure you won't mind if I skip the queue and just pass this to him.' She held out the folder she was carrying.

Gareth called out: 'Come in,' and Margaret pushed open the door. On the threshold she stood as though frozen to the spot, staring at the tall, grey-haired man who had risen to his feet, a slow flush colouring her cheeks and the folder she was carrying slipping to the floor with a clatter.

David Owen-Thomas crossed the room to take her hands in his, gripping them warmly. 'Margaret! After all these years!'

But Meryl wasn't watching the touching little scene. She was watching, fascinated, as Frances Graham swept across the room to embrace Gareth and kiss him on both cheeks.

'Well, darling, and how are you after all this time?' she purred. 'I'll bet you didn't think when you got up this morning that you'd be seeing *me* before the day was out!'

And from the look on his face, she was right! Meryl bent to pick up the spilled papers on the floor, placing them on Gareth's desk and withdrawing from the room. No one seemed to notice her going. She wasn't surprised.

Meryl stayed in bed late on Saturday morning. At eight-thirty Jane brought her a cup of tea.

'This week it's your turn for a little pampering,' she said cheerfully.

'But there's nothing wrong with me,' said Meryl, sitting up in bed. 'I'm just feeling lazy.'

Jane drew the curtains. 'You've had a hectic week, and to tell you the truth I thought you were looking a bit glum last night. Do you fancy talking about it?'

Meryl sipped her tea. 'Call it winter blues,' she said noncommittally.

'Okay, tell me to mind my own business if you like. You don't have to be polite.' Jane looked at her shrewdly. 'It wouldn't have anything to do with the arrival of a certain glamorous lady, would it?'

Meryl pulled a face. 'I heard Gareth come in very late last night and go out again very early this morning. I also understand he changed his weekend duty with Mike, so it looks as though he intends to make a holiday of it.'

Jane nodded. 'You know, of course, that's she's his ex-fiancée? I understand that her marriage to the consultant broke up a year ago. She ran into Gareth's father when she was on holiday in Tenby. He told her all the news about Gareth and she offered to drive him over to see him. I rather got the impression that he hoped they'd get together again.'

Meryl stared at her. 'How did you get to know all that?'

'As a matter of fact your aunt told me at evening surgery last night. She seemed quite excited at seeing Gareth's father again after all these years—said he hadn't changed a bit.' Jane perched on the edge of the bed. 'He's very like Gareth, isn't he? The same rugged good looks—same build too, and he doesn't look anywhere near his age.' She peered at Meryl. 'If I were you I'd watch that Graham woman. Don't let her snitch Gareth from under your nose!'

Meryl stared at her. 'He doesn't belong to *me*. I'm sure he'll do whatever he pleases. There's nothing I can do about it!'

Jane grinned. 'Oh, I think you could if you put your mind to it. You haven't given him much encouragement so far, have you? I hope you haven't left it too late.'

Meryl got out of bed and pulled on her dressing gown. 'I'm sure I don't know what you're talking about.' She looked at Jane. 'What are you doing today? Shall we drive into Northwich—have lunch and look at the shops?'

Jane shook her head. 'Sorry, Meryl. I'd love to, but I promised to go out with Richard. He was so sweet to me last Sunday—nursed me and waited on me hand and foot, so when he asked I couldn't refuse.'

'I see—well, never mind, it was just a thought.' Meryl began to collect her things for the bathroom, musing that Jane seemed the last person to like being waited on. She seemed too independent. Sometimes people behaved very strangely.

'I know—you could come with us,' Jane suggested brightly. 'I'm sure Richard wouldn't mind—after all, you and he are old friends, aren't you?'

'No!' Meryl said hastily. 'I wouldn't dream of it. I'll slip over and spend the day with Aunt Maggie.'

As she went out of the room Jane looked doubtful. 'I wouldn't bet on it,' she muttered, half under her breath.

When Meryl rang the front doorbell at Woodbine Cottage it was Libby who answered the door. Meryl went inside and took off her coat, then she noticed Libby looking at her oddly.

'I thought I'd come and spend the day with you both,' she explained.

'Oh, but your aunt isn't here,' Libby told her. 'She went off early this morning with Mr Owen-Thomas. They're making a day of it. Didn't you know?'

'Of course I didn't. I wouldn't be here if I did!' Meryl's tone was sharper than she intended as she looked at the housekeeper. 'I thought he was here to see his *son!*'

Libby smiled. 'You should have seen her this morning —up with the lark and singing in the bath! Like a girl again, she was. Surely you don't grudge her a bit of pleasure?'

Meryl sighed. 'Of course I don't.' She fell silent, not wanting to admit that what was making her so crestfallen was the realisation that if David Owen-Thomas was with her aunt, Gareth must be spending the day with his ex-fiancée. She managed a smile at Libby.

'Never mind, you and I can have lunch together. It's ages since we had one of our long talks.'

Libby's smile vanished. 'Oh dear—we can't, I'm afraid. You see, as I was free for the day I rang my friend Mrs Mountford and we arranged to go and do some early Christmas shopping.'

'And here I am stopping you from getting ready. Sorry, Libby.' Meryl kissed the housekeeper's cheek. 'I'll see you again soon. Off you go—and have a nice time.'

As she drove the car aimlessly back towards town she felt somewhat out in the cold. Everyone was busy enjoying themselves. No one wanted her, not even Libby, who was usually so pleased to see her. As she neared the centre of Millington she had a thought. Jane had said that Mike Taggart had taken over Gareth's weekend duty, so Jean would be at a loose end. Maybe *she* could do with some company.

She was right—Jean was pleased to see her. She welcomed Meryl into her sunny Victorian kitchen and made coffee for them both. She also had some news.

'Have you heard about the Johnsons?' she asked.

Meryl shook her head.

'They're moving back to Lancashire. Mrs Johnson told me yesterday when she brought her husband for his physio session. It seems the perfect compromise. It seems that Gerald Johnson always wanted to go back to his home town when he retired, and now his wife has agreed. She told me that you arranged for her to do a little voluntary work at the day centre, helping with the disabled. One afternoon there made her see how lucky she was that her husband had made such a good recovery. That was when she decided to go along with his wishes and move back up north.' Jean smiled. 'So it's one up to Meryl Taylor, eh? What with that and your part in the drama of the rig, you're getting to be quite the heroine!'

'I only wish I could sort my own life out as easily,' Meryl said glumly.

Jean frowned. 'Oh dear—like that, is it? Anything I can do?'

Meryl shrugged. 'I confided in you a little a few weeks ago—about Gareth. Things haven't really gone any further between us. Now his ex-fiancée has turned up out of the blue.' She looked at Jean. 'But maybe you heard?'

Jean shook her head. 'No. I understood it was his father who was here for a visit.'

'He is, but this Frances Graham woman came too,' Meryl told her. 'Apparently she ran into Gareth's father and offered to drive him over to see his son. She's divorced now and it rather looks as though Mr Owen-Thomas is hoping to get them together again. I called in at Woodbine Cottage this morning, but Libby tells me Aunt Maggie has gone out with Gareth's father for the day—they're old friends from university days.' She peered gloomily into her cup. 'Obviously that means that Gareth is spending the day with Frances.'

'And you're finding that it hurts more than you expected it to?' Jean enquired. Meryl bit her lip and Jean asked: 'What about Richard? He seems happy enough, in spite of your breaking with him.'

'He and Jane have discovered each other,' Meryl told her. 'The speed at which he's recovered isn't exactly flattering.'

Jean laughed gently. 'Poor Meryl! You know, I think I can understand why Richard is attracted to Jane. She may seem very self-assured, but she's wise enough to know when to appear vulnerable. She makes Richard feel strong and masculine—a feeling he didn't get with you, if you don't mind my saying so, dear. You know, you can be *too* independent, Meryl.'

Meryl looked up at her, slightly dismayed. 'I didn't know I gave that impression. Gareth said he liked a woman to have guts.'

'Having guts and being totally self-sufficient are two very different things,' Jean told her. 'Think about it.' She got up from the table and cleared away the coffee cups. 'Now, I've got this new pattern for an evening dress and I can't make head or tail of it. Perhaps you can help me.'

Meryl's expression was pensive as she washed the cups at the sink. She had plenty of food for thought while Jean was upstairs fetching the pattern.

It was ten o'clock when Meryl left the Taggarts' house. Mike had come in tired and she felt that he and Jean needed to be alone to eat their supper in peace. As she drove she thought about the empty beach house and shrank from the thought of going back there alone. To think that when she had first moved in she had relished the thought of solitude! One could soon get used to companionship, she told herself wryly. She found herself heading for Woodbine Cottage. Libby could make her a bedtime drink; maybe she would even spend the night there.

But as she walked up the path she saw that most of the lights seemed to be on. Aunt Maggie must be home early. She rang the bell. Libby opened the door and immediately she heard the sound of several voices coming from the sitting room. She began to turn away.

'Oh, Aunt Maggie has company. I won't intrude—' But the smiling housekeeper reached out to take her arm, pulling her inside.

'Come in. Your aunt was only just saying she wished you could be here. There's no one here you don't know. It's so exciting! Wait till you hear the news!'

In the hall Meryl took off her coat. The sitting room door was open, and suddenly she saw Gareth and Frances Graham as well as her aunt and Mr Owen-Thomas. Everyone seemed to be holding glasses of what looked suspiciously like champagne. She felt herself burning with embarrassment. If only she had trusted her first instinct and gone away before it was too late! Mr Owen-Thomas suddenly caught sight of her and came out into the hall to welcome her.

'Ah, Miss Taylor—or may I call you Meryl? You're just in time to join the party!'

'Party?' she echoed, staring at him.

He smiled and took her arm. 'That's right. Come along, my dear. You must let me get you a glass of champagne. After all, it isn't every day we have an engagement to celebrate, is it?'

CHAPTER TWELVE

In a daze, Meryl allowed herself to be led into the sitting room. A glass was placed in her hand and she sipped at it—more from the need of a stimulant than in celebration of what she had just been told. It hadn't taken Frances long to regain her place in Gareth's life! How she must be congratulating herself on running into her future father-in-law so fortuitously. Gareth raised his glass and the chatter died down.

'A toast!' he announced. 'To two people who've taken over thirty years to make a dream come true. To the future Mr and Mrs David Owen-Thomas—Margaret and Dad!'

There was a pause as everyone drank—everyone except Meryl. Frances went across to kiss Margaret on the cheek and shake David's hand, while Meryl stared at the scene before her, too numb for words.

'You're looking rather stunned. Wouldn't it be nice to congratulate your aunt?' Gareth was looking down at her. Meryl shook herself out of the stupor of shock she found herself in, looking up into the amused grey eyes.

'I was just about to. It's just such a surprise—I thought—When your father said an engagement, I thought—'

A slow smile spread over his face. 'You didn't think it was *me*, did you?' He threw back his head and laughed. 'Good God!' He glanced round. 'Not that Frances isn't a very beautiful woman, of course. And now that she's free—who knows?'

Meryl made to move away, but he caught at her arm, bending his head to speak quietly to her. 'Would you have been upset if it had been me, Meryl?' he taunted. 'Would it have been a blow to your ego? It would be no more than you deserve really, would it? After all, you can't be a dog-in-the-manger for ever.'

She stared at him, her cheeks flaming. 'I haven't the least idea what you're talking about,' she said hotly.

He laughed. 'Of course you have. You don't believe in marriage, do you?'

'It's a matter of personal choice. I was only expressing my own feelings.' She hesitated, biting her lip, then broke off as she saw her aunt coming towards her, her face wreathed in smiles.

'Meryl darling! What luck, your happening to drop in like this. I don't really know what's hit me yet. David has quite swept me off my feet!'

Meryl looked at her accusingly. 'I thought you hardly knew Gareth's father? You told me—'

Margaret took her arm and led her aside.

'Don't be cross with me, dear. I can confess to you now that David and I were engaged all those years ago, but I broke it off—thought more of my career.' She smiled wistfully. 'I've lived to regret it, and so, it seems, has he.' She sighed. 'I have to admit that when I saw Gareth that day of the interview he quite took my breath away. He could have been David, standing there smiling at me with those grey eyes. And when I thought that I might have been his mother—' Meryl's eyes narrowed.

'That was when you decided to try to throw Gareth and me together, I daresay. What a pity it didn't work!'

Margaret blushed guiltily, but she was saved from further explanation as her future husband came up behind her, slipping an arm around her waist, his face no less radiant than hers.

'Why wait at our age?' he said. 'Margaret wouldn't marry me when we were young, and we've both regretted it ever since. Now we owe it to each other to try to make up for all those lost years.'

Meryl swallowed the lump in her throat. 'I think it's lovely. Congratulations, both of you. When is the wedding to be?'

'As soon as it can be arranged,' David put in before Margaret had time to speak. She laughed.

'See what I mean?'

'Frances will be driving me home again first thing in the morning, then I shall pack and come right back,' David told them. 'I don't intend to let Margaret out of my sight again in a hurry. We still have to discuss what we'll do afterwards, of course—where we'll live and so on.'

Meryl stayed on for a while, but as soon as she decently could she made her excuses and left.

The beach house looked deserted as she let herself in. She felt flat and defeated. It was lovely, of course, about Aunt Maggie and Gareth's father. They made a very handsome couple and she was sure they would be happy. It was Gareth's taunting attitude to her that had disturbed her. Clearly he had tired of her persistent refusals to fall in with his wishes. As she took off her coat she remembered something he had said: 'Frances is a beautiful woman—Now that she's free, who knows?' She visualised his ex-fiancée. He was right—she *was* beautiful. They looked perfect together. Maybe Frances too had realised her mistake in turning Gareth down. It seemed this was a night for second chances—except for her!

She undressed and showered, then, putting on her dressing gown, she went into the kitchen to make herself a hot drink. This felt like a night when sleep would need some inducement.

She was just pouring the milk into the cup when she heard the front door slam, and a moment later she turned to see Gareth standing in the doorway.

'Ah, am I in time for a nightcap?' he asked.

Meryl shrugged. 'I'm sure you're capable of making yourself one. I'm taking this to bed with me.' As she passed him he took the cup from her hands and put it down on the worktop, then he reached behind him and closed the door. She stared at him.

'What do you think you're doing? Give me back my drink and let me pass!'

He shook his head. 'Not till we get something straight. We were having a conversation back there at your aunt's house. I'd like to finish it, please.'

She blushed. 'I—can't remember what it was about now.'

He grasped her shoulders. 'Sorry, Meryl, that won't wash. You remember all right. I was teasing you earlier —now I'm serious. I want to hear what you were about to say.'

Meryl stared at him, a suspicion slowly forming in her mind. 'I think you're just getting your own back, enjoying watching me squirm. You weren't asleep that night in the car at all, were you? You heard every word I said!'

He began to laugh and she struggled to free herself

from his grasp. 'Let me go! You've had your fun. I'm tired and I want to go to bed.'

But his hands were like iron as he held her relentlessly, his eyes searching hers.

'You're right, Meryl, I did hear what you said that night—I was only pretending to be asleep. But I had my reasons. Don't you want to know what they were?'

She sighed. 'I assume you changed your mind. Or maybe all you wanted was an unconditional surrender. After that you weren't interested any more—the fun had gone out of the chase.'

Gareth looked down at her, his eyes widening as his hands dropped from her shoulders. 'You make me sound like a prize rat! Is that really how you see me?'

'Well, how do *you* see *me*?' she challenged.

'I think I started to tell you that night,' he told her. 'To begin with I saw you as a spoiled brat—all histrionics; attractive, but self-willed—a woman I might amuse myself trying to tame. But as time went by I saw that there was more—much more—to you. That was why I couldn't accept your surrender when it came; why there was no victory in it for me. That's why I pretended to be asleep. For once in my life I'd met a situation I couldn't handle.'

'And because of that you've been avoiding all contact with me since.' She looked up at him.

Slowly he nodded. 'If you like, yes. You see, I've been discovering something deeper in myself too. It hasn't been easy coming to terms with it, Meryl, but now I have. I no longer want the kind of relationship I offered —not with you, anyway.'

'That's all right, you needn't apologise—I expected it

anyway, now that you and your ex-fiancée have met again.'

He reached out to take her shoulders again, shaking her gently. 'Damn it, Meryl—I'm *not* apologising! And Frances has nothing to do with this. She and I knew years ago that we were totally unsuited to each other.' He stared down at her. 'Do I have to spell it out for you in words of one syllable? Can't you understand what I'm trying to say? I want to *marry* you!'

They stared at each other for a moment as the words hung almost tangibly in the air between them, then he said angrily: 'All right, that was your cue. Now you can laugh! Now it's your turn.'

'I'm not laughing,' she told him quietly. 'And you needn't think you're the only one to have met a situation difficult to handle. Till I met you I thought I knew exactly where I was going. I thought I didn't need anyone, particularly anyone like you. I thought I was free. Now—'

She looked away, but he lifted her chin with one finger, making her look into his eyes. 'Yes—now? *Say* it, Meryl. I want to hear it.'

She shook her head defiantly. 'Why don't *you*? I thought the Welsh were supposed to be a poetic race!'

He looked down at her for a moment, then he said softly: 'Saying what is in my heart doesn't come easily to me yet, Meryl. But what I feel for you is deep and real. Does it tell you anything when I say that one glimpse of that red hair of yours turns my bones to jelly? That the sound of your voice makes my heart beat faster—that holding you close to me makes me happier than anything else I can think of?' He drew her towards him, his fingers gripping warmly through the thin material of her dressing gown. 'You were dressed like this that night at Wellford House when you took me for a burglar. You've no idea what you did to me even then. That's why I was so tough with you, didn't you guess? I suppose subconsciously I knew then that you were the woman who'd one day make me change my whole way of thinking. I'd no choice but to fight you on that score alone!' He drew her close, resting his chin on top of her head. 'I love you, Meryl—I love your maddening stubbornness, your temper and your pluckiness, as well as your lovely face and body.' He held her a little away to look down at her. 'There, is that poetic enough?'

She reached up to wind her arms around his neck, love for him surging through her, filling every corner of her heart till she thought it would burst. 'Oh, Gareth, I love you too,' she whispered. 'I've known it for some time, but never more than tonight, when I thought I'd lost you to someone else.'

He kissed her long and deeply. His lips left hers to find the hollow of her throat, his fingers setting her senses aflame as they caressed her bare neck and shoulder. Opening the door, he took her hand, smiling down at her. Her heart quickened.

'You once said not here,' she whispered. 'Not in this house.'

He laughed gently. 'Somehow I feel it's different now, don't you?' He bent to put one arm behind her knees, swinging her up into his arms. 'Now that we're engaged.'

And Meryl could do nothing but happily agree.

DISCOVER LASTING LOVE.

True love is everlasting.

Rather like our Nostalgia Collection.

This delightful set of books gives a fascinating insight into the romances of the 30's, 40's and 50's.

Each decade had its own popular writers and we've chosen 3 of our favourites to take you back in time in their own distinctive style.

We've even re-printed the original covers, to create a real collector's item for lovers of romantic fiction.

We think you'll find that times may change, but true love simply improves as years go by.

Available from April 1986.

Price £4.75.